A GOLDEN CIRCLE

To Kathleen —

A Golden Circle

*A Tale of
the Stage and the Screen and Music
of Yesterday and Now and Tomorrow
and Maybe the Day After Tomorrow*

Jerome Lawrence

A novel by
JEROME LAWRENCE

Sun & Moon Press
LOS ANGELES

Sun & Moon Press
A program of
The Contemporary Arts Educational Project, Inc.
a nonprofit corporation
6026 Wilshire Boulevard, Los Angeles, California 90036

First published by Sun & Moon Press in 1993

10 9 8 7 6 5 4 3 2
FIRST EDITION

This book was made possible, in part, through a program grant from
the Andrew W. Mellon Foundation and through contributions to the
Contemporary Arts Educational Project, Inc., a nonprofit corporation.

Cover: Gustav Klimt, *Adele Bloch-Bauer I*
Osterreichische Galerie, Vienna
Design: Katie Messborn
Book design & typography: Jim Cook

LIBRARY OF CONGRESS CATALOGING IN PUBLICATION DATA
Lawrence, Jerome
A Golden Circle
ISBN 1-55713-086-8
I. Title. II. Author.
811'.54—dc 19
CIP

Printed in the United States of America

I.

WHEN Jed looked into her face for the first time, he couldn't believe he was in this room. Young Kati beside him seemed equally awed and excited. "The Divine Rachel" sat in a great chair, a legendary queen of the theater holding court in her Manhattan brownstone mansion.

Was she Dickens' Miss Havisham? A female High Lama of a long-lost Lost Horizon? She was far younger than those fictional centenarians: a near perfect complexion, a voice that never quavered. She spoke with lyric magic, as if there were a 38-piece pit orchestra in her soul.

"Give me your hands," the great lady said. "Both of you."

Jed and Kati walked toward her. When she held their hands, quite tightly, warmth spread through her fingers into theirs. She smiled.

"Your faces are full of question marks. Good. My favorite punctuation. You're both asking: isn't this some impostor, a young understudy or stand-by sent over by Actors' Equity to impersonate me? Of course not. It's public knowledge that I was born on the birth-year of this century. Statistically that makes me 92. But not really. What age would you like me to be? Actually, I'm every year I ever lived. 18 mostly, though occasionally I'm quite fond of 30. At the moment, I'm genuinely enjoying 92."

5

Jed and Kati glanced at each other. Rachel didn't let go of their hands, and they didn't want her to.

"Most people think it's impossible that I'm still alive. But here I am: working and breathing and singing and eating everything I want to eat, and seeing everybody I really want to see, and not seeing everybody I don't want to see."

"Thank you for seeing us."

"I almost didn't when you told me your name. What was it again?"

"Jed Jefferson."

"I'm not sure I approve of it. It's good enough, I suppose, except for the first part and the last part. I hope you have a decent middle name."

"No middle name. Sorry."

"Dear me. I wouldn't like to think of your uncle's nephew as a combination of Jed Harris and Joseph Jefferson. Oh, Jed did a few good things in the theater, *Our Town* especially, but most of the time, he was a theatrical son-of-a-bitch. And of course you know who Joseph Jefferson was; he played *Rip Van Winkle* to death, the way Gene O'Neill's father mummified his career with all that Château d'If nonsense. I'm told that audiences at *Rip* yawned themselves to sleep for twenty years."

"What about calling me Jedediah? It's my legal name; I don't use it because it's a mouthful and doesn't fit on a driver's license."

"Jedediah. That's a mouthful I like. And it doesn't remind me for a minute of Jed Harris."

"About the Jefferson part: why not forget Joseph and slip in Thomas? I like to think I might be vaguely related to or descended from Tom Jefferson."

"You've got some backbone, Jedediah Jefferson. Some spine. I like people who speak up, who talk back to me. I

6

usually terrify youngsters your age. They think of me as some kind of high-school principal. Of course, if I really were a principal, or some high-mucky-muck of education, I'd turn every school into a theater. A matinee every class period whatever they're trying to teach. Dramatize those dull textbooks, shove them onto stages, with music and dancing and especially a lot of laughs. That might open up the ears of all the pupils who've stopped listening, make them realize that history is a helluva comedy and damn good drama too, and that it's a show that goes on and on, and doesn't have to have any final curtain. Now, tell me your name, child."

"Kati. Katherine actually."

"And do you have a last name, Kati-Katherine?"

"Well, sort of. My professional name is Kati Singer."

"And you want to be a singer. No, you already are. Jedediah, turn on a lamp or two. It's getting a bit dusky and I'd prefer looking at your faces in total sunlight."

She let go of their hands. Jed turned on the closest lamp, making the golden walls of the room shimmer with light.

"See?" Rachel marveled. "A tiny lamplight turns the dark into a sunrise. A few more lights and the middle of the night becomes a sunny afternoon. With every lamp in this room on, I'm at the very center of a circle of gold: every midnight turns into noon. More lights, Jedediah, and you'll see what I mean."

Kati helped Jed switch on more lamps and the room became dazzling. "It's beautiful. Is the wallpaper made from golden cloth, or are the walls painted gold?" Kati asked.

"Paint? Wallpaper? Of course not. The walls are covered with pure gold, gold leaf actually. So are the ceilings and the piano; why should they be poor relatives? Now, I

7

don't want you to think of me as some kind of mad-woman-miser, some Midas-like millionaire, which I'm not. Sunshine is the greatest wealth any of us can have; why not use it twenty-four hours a day? And night! You can't *live* with stocks or bonds. And who'd want to paper their walls with them? You have to hide the poor-little-rich things in a vault or a safe-deposit box. They must know how much they're worth, but what good is that kind of wealth when you're locked up and in the dark all the time? How lonely it must be for them."

"Madame Rachel, you're incredible," Jed said, kneeling at her chair. But inside his head he kept asking himself: "What the hell am I doing here, three thousand miles east of nowhere? I'm not exactly sure where I've been, and I sure as hell don't know where I'm going."

But when Kati knelt beside him, Jed was warmed by the glow of gold on her face.

Rachel leaned forward and gently kissed each of them on the cheek.

II.

THE idea of shipping himself east, Kati in tow, hit Jed a few months before in San Francisco. He liked the town even though the pavements he walked still had blurred ravages of earthquakes and fires past, splits in the sidewalks swallowing up footprints. But all the hills headed toward the sky and there were bridges almost everywhere you looked, sculptured against the clouds. He liked the taste of the mist and the fog, blended with the shrimp and bean-sprout smell of sizzling woks.

What Jed didn't like was his job. He covered the alleged entertainment along two city blocks of cacophony he labeled "Noise Street" for a sleazy tabloid called *The Rag*, San Francisco's blood-brother to the *National Inquirer* and *The Star*.

"What we want from you, kid," his editor told him repeatedly, "is horse-shit not hosannas, dirt not church services. Our readers don't give a shit about the size of a broad's voice, just the size of her tits."

The punk rock and heavy metal, masquerading as music, poured out of every *boîte*, bar, converted storefront, hole-in-the-wall, electronic shrine. Every stop was out, buttons and switches and potentiometers shoved to full: loud to louder to loudest, vocal chords blasting every note into a primal scream.

As Jed walked along the street, the noise almost

drowned him with loudness. He closed his eyes for an instant, speculating how wonderful it would be if God, or whoever invented the human animal, had provided us with a turn-off switch for ears as convenient as eyelids. But even some anatomical contraption or man-invented earplugs couldn't have held back the tidalwave of decibles pushing against the red line, sweeping out of every entranceway.

He stopped in front of his night's assignment, a tiny club that prided itself on showcasing new talent. Pretty enough gal on the garish poster, with a hint of post-teen age innocence, but the gussied-up commercial photo made her look assembly line plastic. The painted neon-like letters were designed to scream at you:

KATI SINGER
THE SINGER OF THE CENTURY
THE 21ST!
No Cover. 2 Drink Minimum

The synthesizer, the percussion, and the electric guitar were loud enough to pollute Sausalito. Jed went inside, took his place one table back from ringside, noting that he was the only press coverage there. He unfolded some copy paper and dug out the stub of a pencil. He glanced around at the usual crowd of half-drunk kids with weird haircuts, who cheered and whistled and ordered refills, not only beer but get-high-quick stupid "smart drinks."

Then Kati Singer came on. In the flesh, she was prettier than the poster-shot, tiny, which gave her a childlike quality, yet that compact body never stopped. She motioned to the combo and what came out was more-of-the-same, standard fodder for the customers of Noise Street.

Jed scribbled some notes as the numbers went on and

on: "Kati Singer is a run-of-the-mill screamer with probably not enough vocal power to reach Punk Rock Heaven by the start of the 21st Century. But if you need a cute little chassis to bring on your next wet-dream, you might want to discover her yourself."

Everybody in the room seemed to like the gal until a funny switch happened.

"Turn off the juice, guys," she said. "And, Hank, get over to the piano. I'd like to do one more number."

"We ain't rehearsed one more number, honey."

"Don't need any rehearsal. Just give me a few chords."

"Any particular key?"

"F is friendly."

Shrugging, he moved to the tiny previously unused piano, swung it around, and played a few chords. The unaccustomed softness of the non-electronic music made everybody in the place go into a puzzled silence.

Kati began to sing, half a capella, and migod, Jed could understand the words. It had a melody, sweet, old-fashioned maybe, but it touched his ears like healing balm: a song he'd never heard before, called "Why Did Yesterday Go Away?"

There was quiet in the joint for 16 bars and then the place came apart with hoots and hollers. The connoisseurs of noise got up, slapped bills down for their checks, and waved the others to a joint across the street where, Jed thought, the higher decibles could relieve them from the obligation of talking, of feeling, especially of thinking. But Kati Singer didn't stop singing. Jed slowly tore up the scribbled paragraph of his review. As he watched her, and listened to her voice in the otherwise unexpected silence, he got an erection.

III.

JED stood in the street, watching Kati coming out of the now empty and noiseless club. She had a red scarf over her head and her stance and her stride were more defiant than angry.

"Hey, Ladybird," Jed said, "that was a hell of an opening night."

"Closing night, too. You get 'em both in one hunk."

She kept walking.

"That stupid manager let you go just because those taste-starved assholes walked out?"

"I considered it a compliment."

Jed wasn't following her down the street, just sticking close to her side. She stopped for a moment, studied his face. They had to shout to each other over the blaring bookends of Punk Rock and Heavy Metal, assaulting them from both sides of the street. She pointed a finger at him, a delighted accusation.

"You're the one who didn't walk out."

"Happy claque of one. How about a drink? Or a cup of coffee?"

"No way. I never go out with the customers, even in joints where I'm no longer working."

"I'm not a customer, I'm a critic. Promise not to spit."

"A critic! That's worse. See you around."

This time she ran down the street, a child-like Red Riding Hood outdistancing the wolf.

"Hell, I'm no wolf," Jed tried to convince himself without conviction, but he raced after her, catching up at the the stop-light of the first cross-street.

"Ladybird," he said. "I'm gonna give you a helluva review, especially for that quiet song. But I want to know more about it. And you. Sure you won't have a fifteen minute drink? Ten minutes if you're in a hurry."

"I may sound like a bottle baby, or a *non*-bottle baby, but I don't drink, not even coffee. But if you know anywhere in San Francisco they serve hot chocolate, I'll take you up on that."

Jed got a cab and pointed the driver toward Ghiradelli Square.

After a third cup of hot chocolate Kati warmed up. "I don't know where I came from," she said. "Or where I'm going. I'm kind of a mystery. Especially to me."

"Where'd that song come from? Where can I get a copy?"

"You can't. Neither can I. There aren't any copies."

"Did you hear it someplace?"

"Yeah. In my head."

"Sort of a dream?"

"Nope. Wide awake. I hear it all the time. Something my brain does as a favor to my ears. Tonight I finally decided to sing my thing out loud."

"But *soft* loud, thank you, with words and music complete and copyrighted inside your beautiful head."

"The lyrics aren't always the same. Some days, when I'm particularly pissed-off, the words kinda swear at each other. And the tempo keeps changing. But mostly it's half hymn, half waltz, part nursery rhyme, part 'Down in the Depths on the 90th Floor.'"

"You're a throwback, kid. But I wish they'd throw more beauties like you back."

"I'll bet you're not a bad writer. You sure talk good. Hey, I don't think all this is too crazy. It's like you see those National Geographic things and the natives are always chanting and pounding their drums to make the rain come. But nobody ever comes around with a hymn book or a fancy rock arrangement to tell the tribe what to chant. It's all there, under their skins, like some kind of tribal memory they were born with. Maybe it's the same way with that song."

And Kati kept humming it as they left Ghiradelli Square and climbed a couple of hills to a tiny boarding hotel, where she lived. They shook hands and she thanked him for all the hot chocolates and he thanked her for the song. Before she disappeared through the leaded-glass front door, he called after her.

"Hey, Ladybird! Katydid! Can I see you again? Soon?"

"Hey, Critic-face. I'm not sure."

And she closed the door. At least, he knew where she lived.

IV.

JED'S boss ripped the review of Kati's opening/closing night out of the computer even before Jed finished it. The smelly office of the *Rag* always seemed smelliest when "Fat Phil" edited over his shoulder.

"You expect me to run this crap?" Phil demanded. "That club won't take three inches of ad space ever again if you throw roses at a broad they already fired. What'd you do, Buster, sleep with her?"

Jed got up, started toward the door.

"Lousy to have known you. Lousier to have worked for you."

"Can't you get out of here any faster? Go. Get lost. You're the easiest thing to replace since they invented jockey shorts. Lot of you out-of-work hacks hangin' around, begging to take my money. Or hasn't anybody told you newspapers are disappearing faster than theaters and movie studios?"

Jed reached over to a stack of last week's issue, the covers splashed with headlines about the sex lives of mayors and television stars, basketball players and royal families. He crumbled a copy, made a perfect shot into a wastebasket across the room.

"You call that thing a newspaper? Christ, they shouldn't hawk it at check-out counters of supermarkets. It belongs on the shelves alongside the toilet paper. I take that back. I wouldn't wipe my ass with it."

And he walked out, his rear end saying farewell to his weekly pay check.

When Jed reached his digs, a rented tower room of a furbelowed Victorian house in Pacific Heights, he found two large cardboard boxes addressed to him, dumped just inside the entryway by UPS, signed for by his landlady. A legal-looking envelope in the mailbox was from a quad-ruple-named law firm, postmarked Hartford, Connecticut. He didn't wait to climb to his tower. He sat on the bottom step and ripped open the letter, which gave him an unex-pected, muchly-needed Christmas-in-April. A check enclosed read: $7,243.26 = Final accounting of the estate of Joshua Lewis, deceased.

Jed's fingers fumbled as he unfolded the covering let-ter. He hadn't heard anything about his nearly-unknown Great Uncle for ten years or more, and then only snippets of passing references in Christmas cards or hasty birthday phone calls from his grandmother Naomi, Joshua Lewis' sister. He'd never even met the man.

There were three pages and a folded stamped return envelope. The covering letter read:

Dear Mr. Jefferson:

We regret the delay in sending you this final settlement of the will of your late Great Uncle Joshua Lewis, who passed away in Milford, Connecticut in October of 1990. The pro-bate was somewhat lengthy and the address he had for you, his sole heir, was a faulty one.

Two boxes of what appear to be books were held here in storage until your current address could be determined. Confirmation of that was finally obtained from the Social Security office in Washington, D.C. Previous notices to you, to a variety of addresses in Ohio, New York, and New Orleans, were returned to us unclaimed.

Copies of those provisions of your Great Uncle's will which apply to you are enclosed as an appendix to this letter. Please sign the probate papers, also enclosed herewith, acknowledging receipt of the check as well as the two cartons, which had been personally packed, sealed and addressed to you by Mr. Lewis previous to his death. A convenient SASE is contained herein.

> Sincerely,
> Otis Constazian,
> Attorney-in-fact,
> Estate of Joshua Lewis

A scribbled note by Attorney Constanzian on a yellow Post-it was attached to the next page:

Mr. Jefferson,

This page, originally holographic and hardly in legal language, was finally accepted by Probate as it seems to have been properly witnessed.

> O.C.

The holograph page, translated into a typed copy, made Jed feel as if he'd actually known the man who wrote it:

Article IV.: On the death of my old buddy, my L.C. Smith typewriter, a lifelong member of this family, and since I refuse to graduate to those monster computing-machines which always seem to talk back at me and say: "For Christ's sake, get O'Neill, or at least Robert E. Sherwood," I hope this handwritten portion of my will can pass muster and not be denied by some probate court which relishes getting their filthy fingers up your ass, particularly after you're dead.

Sub-para. A.: I wish to be cremated and have my ashes scattered lovingly along Shubert Alley, where I always wanted to LIVE.

Sub-para. B.: After you've disposed of what sticks of furniture are still vaguely vertical and the few duds still hanging around hangers to the Salvation Armies or Good Wills of your choice, I'd like all else (though "all" is a wild exaggeration) to go to my grand-nephew, Jed Jefferson, wherever the hell he is, especially a couple of boxes of materials which have always inspired me, hoping they will inspire him to higher heights than I have ever reached. Does that put me in the category of a postmortem teacher of a face I have never seen or whose mind I have never known? Maybe.

Jed couldn't read any more. He raced up the stairs, toting the heavy boxes one at a time. When they were both on the floor, dead center of his tower room, he grabbed a knife, and carefully slit open the top of each box. He just stared at the stacks of books and magazines, letting the "mongrel hour" of half-day, half-night settle on them, a benediction of San Francisco dusk. He wanted very much to open the cover of the first book, the tenth book, the fiftieth book, but not yet, not yet, not until his heart stopped beating so fast.

V.

WHEN it became too dark in his tower room to do anything but think and touch, Jed turned on his desk lamp. He lifted out the top item in the first cardboard carton: *Theatre Arts Monthly*, November 1930. A note, marking a page of the magazine, read:

Dear Grand-Nephew-I-Never-Knew:

This is the face of my greatest inspiration, though I only knew her six months of my life, and never after that, except at an adoring distance. I hope you will meet her some day, some way, somehow, though by now she'll probably be a very old young lady.

Grand-Unk Joshua

An entire page of the magazine contained a photograph full of beautiful shadows, with the key lighting on the high cheekbones of an actress. Her eyes were subtly made-up to suggest she was playing an oriental and her costume seemed threaded with Chinese gold. The caption under the photograph read:

RACHEL (Formerly RACHEL REGINE) in the title role of THE MANDARIN LADY (Act I), a first-play by Joshua Lewis, at the Belasco. This theatrical fable had the shortest run in recent Broadway memory: four performances.

Jed didn't even look at the other books and periodicals, some tattered, some mint-fresh, all with markers stuck in pages by an uncle he never realized had once been a playwright.

Jed spent the rest of the evening staring at the face on that page in *Theatre Arts* of a long-ago November. Mesmerized by a photograph, he forgot to eat dinner.

* * *

The next day, he left a note at Kati's hotel:

Ladybird! I've got some hot news for you. Yesterday hasn't gone away—not entirely. I'd like to show you a sample. How about meeting me today at the Embarcadero around ten minutes to 5:00, which will give us time enough to get to the top deck of the Sausalito Ferry, heading for a hunk of sunset? If you've never taken that ride, I think you'll find it's a hell of a trip. What I'll have under my arm may prove to be a trip for you, too.

> Your un-deaf chum,
> Jed

She was there, five minutes early, her hair loose in the April wind, no hair spray which had made it look plasticized in the cubby-hole nightspot. She took his arm, not saying anything, as they headed for the ticket window. Under his other arm, Jed clutched the issue of *Theatre Arts Monthly*.

The ferryboat chugged out into the Bay. By the time Kati and Jed reached the open upper deck, the panorama of seven hills, matched no place else on earth but Rome, spread out before them.

"Why haven't I ever taken this boat ride before?" Kati marveled.

"You didn't have me to take you."

An old man with a battered banjo began plunking away, a tipped-over cap on the deck alongside him, awaiting quarters, maybe even dollars. He began to sing of San Francisco, a timeless city, hugging the bay and the sky. Clutching the railing, Kati and Jed sang along, phrase after phrase.

Jed tossed a dollar into the banjo-man's cap, then pulled her to a seat beside him on the paint-peeling ferryboat bench. Jed opened the magazine. "You know who this is?"

"No, I don't think so. Hey, wait a minute. Sure, I know her. That's Rachel. Madame Rachel."

"That well, huh? First name basis."

"No, I don't mean I know her. I know who she is. I never met her. And I didn't know she had that last name. Regine? Doesn't that mean 'queen' or something?"

"You have any idea where she might be? Where I can find her?"

"God, no. I always wanted to meet her, maybe even study with her. But I guess I missed that boat. She can't still be around. If she is, she's got to be older than God. How old is that magazine?"

"1930. November issue."

"That's even before my parents were born, if I ever had any parents."

Jed didn't ask any questions about that strangely cryptic statement. The boat veered leeward as it passed Fortress Alcatraz so that the dipping sun hit Kati squarely in the face. He held the magazine closer to her eyes.

"Have a look at her cheekbones, then have a look at yours."

"I can't do both, Critic-face, unless you hang a mirror around your neck. Your chest doesn't reflect."

"Do all singers and actresses want to have bone-structures like hers—and yours?"

"But it doesn't always come naturally, so we spend hours and hours squeezing our cheeks, trying to make the bones grow upward. And lots of facial massages, palms pushing cheek skin up, chin to hairline. All to make ourselves look as much as possible like movie stars, who don't have to do all that because they've already got 'em."

She jokingly pinched her face with her fingers to illustrate the technique, then burst out laughing. Jed was so taken with her caper that he kissed her smack on the right cheekbone.

"Want to try the left one?"

"Sure. I'm adventurous. I'll try anything twice."

He held her this time, his hand with the magazine around her shoulder. The left cheekbone kiss was more gentle. The banjo-man applauded and started plunking out a sentimental tune.

"Why are you trying to find out about Madame Rachel?" Kati asked, taking the magazine. "That's all they called her on the cover of the book she wrote."

"Book?"

"*How to Act a Song.* I never used to like anything anybody ever said 'you have to read' or that'll 'do you a world of good.' But if it's possible to bless a nun, I sure as hell blessed Sister Maria at the convent for *making* me read Madame Rachel's book. How can anybody be a star in the musical theater or in the movies without reading it? Or studying with her. I heard once that Madame took students, or used to, not like a class or anything, but just one or two at a time, never charging them or anything, just spilling out all kinds of things they oughta know, not just to singers, but actors and even playwrights and directors, and she made a lot of stars start to be stars."

"Is that what you want to be—a world-famous star? Stage? Screen? Television? Stereoptican slides? Advance technology not even dreamed of in your philosophy?"

"Instantaneously."

"Whoa, Ladybird. You're doin' just fine. But I doubt if you can get into Screen Actors Guild as easily as getting into the Girl Scouts. Or pour water over yourself, holy or otherwise, and bubble up as fast as instant oatmeal."

"You're a pessimist, Critic-face."

"Not really. Though I think to get a job as a critic on most newspapers these days you have to sign some kind of loyalty oath that henceforth and forevermore you'll remain vicious, demeaning and denegrating. Okay. Spleen all spent. Now. What's all this convent jazz? You don't seem like a person I'd tell to 'Get thee to a nunnery.'"

"Nobody ever told me to 'get thee' anywhere. I just happened to be there when I was old enough to realize I was anywhere."

"Were you sort of a foundling? Or did that word go out with Dickens?"

"I don't think the sisters—oh, there are a few brothers there, too, not *my* brothers, if I ever had any, but priest-like brothers, real great guys, I even fell in love with one of them, a lot of good that did me. Well, they would never tell me where the hell I came from, though about every Tuesday and Thursday they'd say I was heading straight for hell, but I don't think any of them 'found' me, I got the impression I was sorta dropped off there, or delivered there in swaddling clothes, there's another Dickens word for you. But I never minded because it was a pretty swell place, a non-orphanage kinda orphanage about fifty miles north of here right near the ocean. I guess I got special treatment because lots of money kept arriving for the place and for me with never any return addresses on the envelopes, and lots of toys and clothes, which the sisters made me share with the other kids. But I really started to enjoy the place just about the time I was diving head-first into puberty and Sister Maria arrived there."

Kati's rush of words, fresh and unfettered as the wind off the ocean, made Jed miss the fact that the ferryboat had docked at Sausalito, that a load of passengers had disembarked and a whole new set had crowded onto the decks; the boat was now in reverse gear, heading back to the Embarcadero.

"Sister Maria? Wasn't Maria a character in *Sound of Music*?"

"Yup. That's where she got the name. She played the part at Bishop Heelan High School in Sioux City, Iowa, and she liked it so much that when she joined up she asked them to let her have that name like always. Her original name was Gert Brinkerhoff, so I don't blame her."

"What was your name originally? Is Kati Singer a stage name?"

"You call that joint you caught me in a *stage*? 'Course it's a made-up name, the last part anyhow, but nobody told me I ever had a last name, I don't think they really knew. So at the convent, they always just called me Katherine, figuring I'd grow up to be 'Sister Katherine' and wouldn't need a last name at all, so why bother? I started calling Sister Maria 'Gert' for laughs, when none of the other sisters were listening, and it was Gert who helped me pick out a last name for me. She told me about a family in Iowa, whose grandfather had a long German name nobody on Ellis Island could understand, so they asked him what his occupation was, and he said 'Schneider' which means tailor, and that's how the Schneider family got their name. Gert said since I was primarily a singer, why not just call me Kati Singer? And I said 'Fine—just so nobody thinks I'm a sewing machine.' Gert was a real kick, not like any kind of holy sister ever anywhere. She was an O.C.A. freak and she turned me into one."

"What's an O.C.A. freak?"

"An original cast-album maniac. When Gert first arrived at the convent, she had an old suitcase full of Broadway show albums and she shoved it under her cot and never showed anybody but me what was inside it. She told all the sisters and brothers that they were family heirlooms. A couple of times a month Gert managed to get the convent van and said we were going on a mission to some old California mission, but we'd really buzz off to Santa Rosa where there was a record shop with a glassed-in listening booth, and we'd pretend to want to buy some lousy new album, which we never did, and we made like we were hearing it rapturously. Gert always had a couple of her own favorite old O.C.A.'s tucked under her habit and we'd put them on and Gert would usually sing-along and when I learned all the lyrics I'd sing-along too and at the end of each side of each LP, we'd take elaborate bows and applaud each other. The record store owner must've figured out what we were doing since we never bought anything, but he didn't seem to mind, especially when Gert found out he was a non-practicing Catholic and she promised him she'd say a lot of Hail Marys for him. Hey, I gotta tell you something Gert did one day, right there in that listening-booth, after we'd heard an overture on one of the albums. Gert always said an overture of a Broadway musical, to be any good, had to be orchestrated so it lifted the top of your head right off till it hit the roof of the theater. She stopped the album and stood there kinda transfixed, and her face looked as if she were going through some kind of transfiguration. And she said, soft, almost as if she were saying a prayer: 'As a Sister of Mercy, I'm supposed to love God and love Jesus, and of course I do. But I don't think God or Jesus minds if I also love Rodgers & Hammerstein and Cole Porter and Lerner & Lowe and Frank Loesser and Bock & Harnick and Jerry Herman and Kander & Ebb.'"

The boat bumped against the wooden pilings of the Embarcadero pier. Kati had a half-smile on her face and a touch of tears in her eyes.

"I talk a lot, don't I? Thanks for listening to my spiel, Critic-face. Now you know why I don't want yesterday to go away."

She hurried toward the narrow iron steps but swung around as she grasped the hand-railing.

"Oh. If you ever figure out if Madame Rachel is still around and you get to see her—even for five minutes—I'd sure as hell like to come along, even if she's as far away as New York, or as close as La-La Land. I've got my own carfare. If you could swing that, I'd kiss you someplace more center-face than your cheekbones."

She went down the steps and across the wooden-planked exitway. Jed let her go, knowing absolutely he'd see her again. Soon.

VI.

JED spent the next two days trying to find a copy of Madame Rachel's book. No San Francisco library had it. One old librarian remembered that their muchly used copy had been pilfered and never returned, but that was a long time ago. Bookshops went immediately to *Books in Print* but found no listing under R for either Rachel or Regine, and nothing under the title, *How to Act a Song*. Jed decided to try the Theater Department over the bridge at U.C. Berkeley.

Out of a locked cabinet, they handed Jed a well-worn volume, cautioning him it was not to be circulated, that it was one of their treasures, and that he should handle it with care, not leaving the room. Jed sat at a long library table, feeling a touch of unaccustomed reverence as he turned to the title page. He wrote down the name of the publisher; only later did he discover not only that the book was out of print, but that the publisher had long since gone out of business.

Then he began to read Rachel's words, unable to stop. Far more than a simple "How To" book, it was filled with affectionate advice: how a ballad was usually a love song, the singer was its lyric messenger; it must be sung one-to-one, not to empty air, or the message would never be delivered. And there was humor on every page, witty descriptions of the "point songs," the comic relief numbers, so necessary to leaven the sentimentality. Every astute composer and lyricist knew they must place the "point" at the end of a line, and the singer and conductor were happy collaborators in supplying the luftpause, which let the audience rush in to fill it with their willing laughter, such a vital part of every comedy song. And clarity, please, and diction! What was the point of a point song if the audience didn't get the point?

And there were tricks of the trade, learned at the feet of masters of musical staging like George Abbott, who could turn a number which "didn't seem to be working" into a show-stopper by subtly raising the lights, and by moving the chorus closer and closer to the audience. Rachel discovered that she could turn up the light power inside herself as a song reached its climax, and that she could stand still as she took stage and yet get closer to her audience by imperceptibly raising her heels off the stage floor.

Rachel's book was alive with pertinent impertinences and irreverent irrelevancies from her earlier days: how Sigmund Romberg, whose melodic operettas like *The Student Prince* ran nearly forever, would occasionally take a baton and conduct the pit orchestra himself. "There are only two tricks to conducting," Rommy would say. "You have to start when the musicians start, and stop when the musicians finish." And he would shake all over with laughter until the buckle of his size 56 belt almost popped apart. And there were wild tales of the prolific Rudolf Friml, whose *Rose Marie* and *Vagabond King* and *The Firefly* ignited Broadway's operetta stages. The dapper Rudy would invariably arrive at rehearsals or opening nights, a lovely oriental maiden on each arm, always a pair, usually sisters, giggling, delicate flesh and blood chinoiserie book ends.

Jed knew he had to meet Madame Rachel, not only because his great-uncle had suggested it, but to get closer to Kati, who also wanted to touch souls with this incredible woman. Back home, he called his old friend, Ed Hastings, at American Conservatory Theatre, asking if he knew if the Divine Rachel in person still kept her store open. Ed promised to phone a former A.C.T. actress who had studied privately with Rachel a few years back, before graduating to stardom in Hollywood. He'd try to find out from her if there were still signs of life from the legendary golden living room in Manhattan and maybe even a working phone number.

While awaiting word from Ed Hastings, Jed dug into his inherited cartons. Both cardboard boxes contained stacks of hardback published plays, monolith monuments from the days when caring publishers still brought out handsome editions of almost every current produced play. Atop the stack was another note from the sender, obviously written with some passion:

Read these plays, kid. Aloud, so you taste the dialogue in your mouth. They're plays that work, pragmatically, on a living stage. On top of that, they're all plays written in my lifetime, not by me, alas, but ones I wish I had written. I'm sending you these because your Grandmother Naomi told me you flirted with writing a few one-act plays when you were a senior in high school in Cleveland and up through your sophomore year in college, when you switched to newspapering. Naomi wrote me not long before she died that you're a hell of a writer, and she ought to know, because she was the best writer of the lot of us, never anything published, no plays, no novels. But journals! Diaries! Letters! All pure poetry and drama and comedy, and she had the rare knack of knowing how to tell a joke on paper!

When I used to compliment Naomi on what a great story teller she was, she'd say, "There's only one thing a good story teller needs: a good listener." And she always said that you, Jedediah, were the best listener of all, even when you were six years old. If you want to do her honor, go back to writing plays. Plays! Plays! Lots of them! A body of work if possible, but at least one play that has passion and purpose in it, and it will make you and Naomi immortal. I'm convinced that writing genius is in the genes, and the burst of talent, the fever in the blood, comes down to you, inherited from the incomparable Naomi. Not from me, I hope. If there's one drop of me that managed to sneak into your creative bloodstream, leech it out—for I was party to a colossal stage disaster and became what somebody once labeled merely a "playwrote." Maybe the stuff in these cartons will point you toward some of the roads I meant to take and the mountain-tops I never reached in my ex-lifetime.

I embrace you from distant places, but a shred of me may still be close at hand. Are you still listening? Start writing that play!

Your hopeful G. Uncle J.

One by one, Jed slowly fingered the published plays, feeling a pulsebeat in each of them: lots of Shaw and O'Neill, Thornton Wilder and Clifford Odets, Maxwell Anderson and Philip Barry, Pirandello and Christopher Fry, Elmer Rice and Robert E. Sherwood, Lillian Hellman and S.N. Behrman, Sidney Kingsley and Kaufman & Hart, Saroyan and Robert E. Sherwood, and in the second carton plays of the late '40s and mid-'50s: Tennessee Williams and William Inge, Garson Kanin and Robert Anderson, Arthur Miller and Paddy Chayefsky, down to the early plays of Edward Albee and even Lawrence & Lee. Jed swore he was going to read every one of them. Aloud. Several times.

The phone rang. Ed Hastings gave Jed Madam Rachel's unlisted Manhattan phone number.

* * *

Kati and Jed flew the Red Eye, which left San Francisco at 10:15 P.M. and was due to snooze into New York's JFK at 6:00 A.M., for God's sake, Kati protesting clear across Arizona and New Mexico and well into Texas. "How can I face life that early in the morning? A lady-of-the-theater properly gets up, in the words of Auntie Mame, every day at the crack of noon!"

Jed had insisted they fly as inexpensively as possible, though he found out later, but never told Kati, that the rates had bumped up to astronomical heights even on the Red Eye.

When Kati had wanted to fly First Class DeLuxe or some transcontinental equivalent of the Concorde, Jed pointed out that he only had "limited funds."

"Well, *my* funds are unlimited, and I think I should spread my manure around, like Thornton Wilder says: it helps young people to grow. Me."

"Katydid, nobody has unlimited funds, and with the price of theater tickets and hotel rooms and restaurant meals and even a daily newspaper, millionaires can be wiped out in weeks. We've agreed that we'd each pay our own way. Of course we'll team up and put together our brains and our talent and maybe even our bellybuttons."

"Slow down on the bellybutton part, Critic-face."

But she put her head on his shoulder and smiled cozily as if figuring out what kind of nice dream to have.

"Hey," Jed asked, not minding at all the closeness of her hair and his bird's-eye view of her cheekbones, "where does all that unlimited moola come from, if you don't mind my asking?"

"Some still unknown Daddy Warbucks—or maybe it's a Mama Warbucks or both—send monthly checks, cashier's checks with no names on 'em except the bank signatures, and they kept coming, even after I checked out of the convent. I always send the Sisters forwarding addresses and they send that moola on to me religiously, which I guess is part of their religion. Always made me feel like Pip in *Great Expectations*—here comes Dickens again—who always thought old Miss Havisham was his 'unknown benefactor'—isn't that a nice thing that should happen to everybody no matter who your fairy-benefactor really turns out to be in the end like Abel Magwitch or somebody crazy like that—but I never found out who mine was and only God knows who he or she or it or they really are. And if God didn't get around to telling me while I was still in the convent, I guess I'll never find out. Oh. For my forwarding address in New York, I told the sisters I'd be at The Algonquin."

"I can't afford to stay there."

"Don't want to be a kept man, huh? You wouldn't be that if we leave out the bellybutton part."

And she fell sweetly to sleep on his shoulder. Jed glanced back: the couple behind him had awakened from their transcontinental attempt to sleep and were leaning forward, listening wraptly to Kati's marathon bedtime story. The woman winked at Jed and the man made the universal hand sign for "Nice going, guy!"

There was some dawn light as they flew over what was probably Ohio, Jed figured. When he looked thousands of feet down, the landscape seemed to be moving westward as his Ohio family had done a lot of years before. Jed had always been told at school that a generation meant a time span of thirty-three years, but here, now, high above his home state, he had the curious feeling that all the generations were blending together, as if the '30s and the '60s and the '90s were all happening simultanously, leapfrogging time just as the plane was leapfrogging landscapes.

VII.

"I'M glad you children are staying at the Algonquin," Rachel said to Kati and Jed, still holding court in her golden living room. "But I hope it hasn't changed too much since the Japanese bought it. It seems appropriate, though. That's where I first started going oriental myself."

"In the title role of *The Mandarin Lady.*"

"Good God, how did you know about that?"

"A photograph of you in *Theatre Arts Monthly.* November 1930."

Softly Rachel muttered "1930," leaning her head back on her throne-like chair, as if trying to find that year, way back then, on her golden ceiling.

"I saw that picture of you, too, Madame Rachel," Kati said. "How beautiful you were." Then quickly, worried that she'd babbled a compliment that was unflatteringly past tense, she added, "But you're even more beautiful now."

Rachel let her mind and her eyes climb down from the ceiling. She smiled at Kati. "Of course I am, child. When you're very young, your face is what nature and genetics hand you. When you're 40 or 60 or even over 90, your face is entirely your own fault. If you've managed to be even slightly beautiful inside all those years, out it comes for all the world to see."

"No wonder my Uncle Joshua wanted me to meet you."

"Your uncle, of course. Your uncle Joshua Lewis. No, he's your great uncle or grand uncle, which is it? In my life, at least the 1930 part of it, he was both: grand and great. He wrote that play for me, did you know that?"

"I only found out a couple of weeks ago. That's why I phoned you from San Francisco. And I think that's why you let Kati and me come see you here."

"Of course. I don't let everybody into this room. But you're the grand, great nephew of Joshua Lewis, who gave me that beautiful play, who wrote it for me as an act of love, three acts actually. But I turned out to be the only one who loved it back. When it closed faster than it opened, I guess Joshua felt it was all his fault, that he'd given me the only failure I'd ever had. And he ran away, God knows where, and I never saw him again, or even heard from him. Until now. And you."

Feeling she was getting soupily sentimental, she waved away the memory. "I'm a tough old bird. I should try to forget a lot of things, or at least not remember them quite so often." But she grasped Jed's hand. "Do you still see him?"

"I've never seen him."

"Do you hear from him?"

Jed, hesitating for a breath, said: "Only in his will. And notes and letters to me along with it. Mainly about you."

She closed her eyes. "In his will. I wish people wouldn't keep going away. Why did yesterday go away?"

Kati shivered and threw her arms around Jed from the back. Jed felt his heart begin to pound. Rachel opened her eyes.

"Is anything wrong, children?"

Kati broke away from Jed and knelt at Rachel's feet.

"It's you, isn't it? You're my Miss Havisham."

"Who? Miss who?"

35

"Havisham, like in *Great Expectations*, but it was actually old Abel Magwitch. You're one or the other, aren't you? And your lawyers or your bank have been sending me checks for years and years to the convent and then to my hotel in San Francisco and pretty soon they'll be coming to the Algonquin. But why have you been doing it? I never did you any great favor, I think, like bringing you food to the graveyard, except maybe that I practically memorized your really great book, which taught me how to act a song, and then I told everybody I knew about it. And how else would you know the title of that song I never heard except in my head?"

Rachel dropped Jed's hand and took Kati's. "I missed most of that, dear child. You must take some lessons in pacing. What I managed to digest of that towering babble of words was that you have the impression I've been sending you checks of some kind, but I don't think I have been. In my too often penurious but occasionally prosperous years on this planet, I've shipped out as much love as possible to persons known and unknown, but rarely cash. So I'm certainly not your Miss Havisham or your what-was-his-name? Mr. Mag-something?"

Welcome silence filled the golden room. Jed and Kati stared at each other, neither believing all this was happening. Rachel leaned forward as if to get out of her chair.

"What we need is music, to take us away from ourselves and bring us back to ourselves. Help me to the piano. I walk beautifully by myself, of course, but I always welcome the strong arms of young people. Younger people."

As they moved toward the piano, they saw for the first time that atop the golden belly of it were silver-framed pictures of theater and musical greats.

"Come," she said. "Sit with me on the piano bench. One on either side. If life isn't musical, what good is it?"

They sat alongside her as she touched the piano keys lovingly, improvising a melody, full of whispers.

"You play so beautifully," Jed said.

"Isn't it wonderful that everybody, like you just did, Jedediah, calls playing the piano 'play'? Of course it is! Wouldn't it sound awful if it was hard work? A piano has to be touched gently, as you would a lover. You must always make love to it."

And she did.

"What do you call that?" Kati asked.

"Nothing. And everything. Improvisation by the yard. Sometimes a waltz. A march backwards in time. A love poem to a time and place where my life really started. Maybe a good title would be: *Opus Minus Sixty-Five.*"

Yesterday didn't ever really go away, Kati told herself, it was just shut up for awhile. Now Rachel's liquid piano variations were painting the whole century golden, matching the luminescence of this room.

"I wish I could sing all those melodies," Kati said. "Are there words, lyrics?"

"Many. And you've already sung them all. Often. In many lifetimes. And so have I. Did you know that I started out as an ingénue in most of their operettas?"

She pointed affectionately to the backsides of the silver picture frames atop the piano. "I played Mitzi, who fell in and out of love with Franz Schubert, in the twelfth company of Rommy's *Blossom Time.* The 'falling out of love' part was what made Schubert not finish that symphony. So, you see, it was all my fault. In case you innocents don't know, that roly-poly, crazy, wonderful bowl of schmaltz in the frame on my far right is Sigmund Romberg. And that's Rudy Friml, the marvel from Bohemia, who wrote more notes of music than Mozart ever would have, even if he hadn't died so young. I finally got to

37

Broadway, singing a lot of the Friml ditties Jeanette MacDonald eventually yodeled at Nelson Eddy in the movies."

Kati touched Rachel's arm and Jed put his arm around her shoulder, both wanting to get closer to her, warmed by the music and the past, intoxicated as if with heady May wine.

"And of course," Rachel went on, "there were all the oom-pa-pa imports from Vienna, Johann Strauss the Younger and Franz Lehar, with their Sacher-torten-pastry plots and their whipped cream waltzes. But!"

She dropped her hands from the keyboard. "I was doing eight performances a week in some operetta fluff, living in a tiny room at the Algonquin, when I suddenly graduated to what everybody called 'The Real Living Theater.' And you know who helped with my commencement exercises? All those marvelous, madmen and madwomen of the Algonquin Round Table who decided to adopt me. They were all the meat-and-potatoes of the theater world and they declared unanimously that it was time I stopped being the meringue on the pastry cart."

Rachel lifted her fingers in the air, like a concert pianist, and struck some triumphant chords, then moved into a lilting melody which sounded like one of those great overtures Kati'd heard in a glass-enclosed booth in Santa Rosa.

"I didn't know your Uncle Joshua then, nobody did; he was making himself as invisible as possible on the fringes of all that wit and spotlighted brilliance, as a busboy for God's sake. He told me later he was also moonlighting as a part time clerk at the Dramatists Guild, so he could be as close as possible to playwrights who were actually writing plays and not just talking about them."

The piano music became more passionate, helping

with their time transportation: Jed and Kati imagined themselves at the outskirts of the Oak Room of the Algonquin, never looking at a calendar, but knowing absolutely they had arrived at the stroke of 1930.

But Jed vaguely resembled Joshua Lewis then, pretending to fill water glasses over and over again, even if they didn't need refills, so he wouldn't miss a scrap of the lyric anecdotes, the dueling of language, the one-upsmanship of mouths poised to open so they could top the penultimate quip.

And Kati, wearing what didn't look like her face at all, was an imagined hatcheck girl, bending her ear out of the entryway checkroom, leaning outside of the double pile of already checked homburgs and fur collared coats, making sure they didn't muffle a syllable of the literate fugue which rose like music from the circumferance of the magic circle in that polished and burnished oak paneled room.

VIII

THE Algonquin Round Table resembled a mini-comic opera. F.P.A., the redoubtable columnist of the *New York World*, invariably arrived first. He seemed to be singing an interior soliloquy, his solo performance augmented by the sound of his uncapped fat red Waterman fountain pen scratching a counter melody on his folded copy paper. A cigar tucked neatly beneath his mustache, he awaited the others, counting on them to help fill tomorrow's "Conning Tower" column. He hoped that Dotty Parker would bring along a new verse he could print, and that all parties forthcoming would have fodder for his Friday column, "The Diary of Our Own Samuel Pepys," on the *World*'s popular Editorial-Opp. page.

His solo to himself and to his copy paper, often in unintentional rhymed couplets, turned into a duet as the shiny-domed Marc Connelly deposited a cloak and a fedora with the young mistress of the cloak-room.

"Gangway!" F.P.A. shouted, imitating the stentorian tones of the stage's Angel Gabriel. "Gangway for de Lawd God Jehovah's Boswell."

Marc Connelly took his seat at the Round Table, attempting humility, but not at all unhappy that his prizewinning hit at the Mansfield was being trumpeted. Their overlapping jibes, jabs, and comic compliments turned into a conversational "round," each only half-listening to the other. The Bard of McKeesport always cupped his right hand behind his ear, so he wouldn't miss a syllable, especially of what he himself was saying. He was pleased when F.P.A.'s fat red pen went to work, scribbling down something Marc had just said.

"The Pulitzer board should have given you a prize for *directing*," F.P.A. said. "How the hell did you ever manage to give notes to de Lawd God Jehovah?"

"Easy as rarin' back and passin' a miracle. When a playwright doesn't have some self-proclaimed Lawd-of-de-universe director screwing up his creation, we do just fine, when we do it ourselves. Garden of Eden climate, Frank, with no serpents in sight."

"Have a cup of b'iled-custard firmament while we're waiting for the others," F.P.A. suggested. "And tell me, Marcus my boy, "what did *Green Pastures* gross this week? I won't publish it, I'll leave that to *Variety*. I'm just curious."

But when Marc quoted the S.R.O. box-office figures at the Mansfield, F.P.A. jotted them down.

The duet became a trio with the arrival of Dorothy Parker, her hairdo resembling her poodle's. Her outstretched hand offered Adams a muchly scratched out verse, scribbled on a sheet of blue stationary from the Hotel Volney. F.P.A. hummed his approval of her lilting verse about constant jilting by assorted gentlemen: a slice of romance-on-wry. Imagined underscoring would have been a blending of a tinkling little girl nursery rhyme tune and a distant sad and lonely cello solo.

Heywood Broun, paunch first, turned them into a quartet. It was no wonder everybody said he looked "like an unmade bed." Everything about Broun seemed unmade, except his mind.

"Aren't you happy, Heywood," F.P.A. glowed, "that

the so-called newspaper, which shall remain nameless in my mouth, fired you simply because you started the Newspaper Guild? You've been freed from that narrow cubby hole of journalism to spread your writing wings in the wide, wide world of *The World*."

All hands felt like applauding. "And we're all going to become millionaires," F.P.A. added. "Due to the influx of such literary home run hitters, circulation has blossomed. Starting tomorrow the newstand price of *The World* drops drastically from 3 cents to 2 cents! That's a total saving for each of us of $3.25 a year, with an added saving in leap years!"

Then everybody did applaud, and Marc Connelly, current practitioner of legends of heaven, leaned forward to ask Broun a question.

"Tell your fellow-chroniclers of the human mind and imagination, Mr. B., where you think your buddies Sacco and Vanzetti are residing at the moment. Heaven? Hell? Or one in each?"

"Oh, I know everybody thinks I'm writing about them too often," Broun answered with sensitive dignity. "But I'm just trying to get them out of Limbo or Purgatory and back where they belong: in the combined consciences of American minds, if any."

Changing the subject F.P.A. flipped his copy paper and poised his chubby red pen for the answer to a more personal question. "And how do you feel about Mrs. Broun being president of the Lucy Stone League?"

"Careful what you call her, Frank. She's Ruth Hale, now and always. We're still legally married, of course, and our 12 year old Woody is as legitimate as hell, thank you. But Ruth even uses her maiden name on her passport these days. Call her Mrs. *Anybody* and she'll come at you with the entire female population as a weapon."

"*Suffrage little women to come unto thee*," *Mrs.* Parker said.

Robert Benchley appeared, curiously silent in contrast to his customary effervescence, not quite ready to turn their conversational cantata into a quintet. He smirked a bit, with the look Dotty described as "a combination of Mona Lisa and Peck's Bad Boy." Everybody knew he was trying to think of a fresh capsule description of a play he hated. His copy was due across the street at the *New Yorker* at 4:00 and it had to be better than last week's rather limp "Oh, God!"

Nor did George S. Kaufman ever compose immediate comic music. He arrived in the Oak Room, scowling over his eyeglasses in bushy-haired silence. But his rare mots were as stiletto-sharp as every working playwright's longed-for perfect Act II curtain line. All the members of the Table Round recalled the time Mr. Lee Shubert appeared at the back end of the Broadhurst while George was in rehearsal for his latest play. Shubert-the-Elder shouted across the empty seats: "What you need for that Act II curtain is a very funny line!"

"As for example, Mr. Shubert?" Kaufman replied.

Alexander Woollcott always took up the rear, not his own rear, George-the-K always noted; it would take a huge derrick or giant crane to move that enormous butt across the Algonquin lobby. Aleck was the Grand Pooh Bah of the place, but nobody minded his taking over because they all loved his philosophy of criticism, especially when he was the *Times* then the *World* critic and he "tossed his hat in the air"—though his occasional pan of a play or a person could hit you in the balls harder than a croquet mallet.

Aleck often brought along his "discovery," Harpo Marx, and everybody loved him as much as Woollcott did.

Dotty Parker noted that Harpo didn't have to bring his heavy harp with him; his silence and his sweet, half-naughty smile made pure harp music.

Other Johnnies-come-sometimes included playwright and later FDR speechwriter Robert E. Sherwood, so tall that Harpo would pantomime to him to duck as he crossed the lobby so he wouldn't brush his head and his haircut on the ceiling fixtures. Edna Ferber, silenced into humility, believed she could match the brilliance of the others on the printed page, but never as an in-the-flesh, spontaneous master of the unrehearsed ad-lib, unless she'd carefully rehearsed it beforehand,

The Lunts occasionally dropped in, on non-matinee days of course, listening from the edges. Once Alfred said urgently: "Quick, somebody, write it all down—so some day Lynn and I can pretend on stage that *we* made it all up ourselves.

And F.P.A. kept writing, not for the Lunts but for his "Conning Tower" column, never even taking the cigar out of his mouth to use as an exclamation point.

The ensemble climax of this civilized cacophony seemed to those lucky enough to be within hearing distance to be a symphony of wit.

IX.

AT her golden piano in her golden room, Jed and Kati at either side of her, Rachel shared and relived her borning moments as a dramatic actress. Clear of eye and voice in the '90s as she had been in her '20s, Rachel shouted the praises of those unbeatable Round Table conversational Olympic champions "who talked me into the rest of my life."

It had been Woollcott who took the young Rachel's arm as she emerged from the Algonquin's claustrophobic elevator into the lobby, and wordlessly led her to the Round Table. Everybody stood up and applauded.

Woollcott remained standing as Rachel and all the others took their seats. Alec seemed like a king about to tap a sword on her shoulder, declaring her a Dame-of-the-Realm. "We've all watched you with delight, Miss Regine, in the musical playhouses of Manhattan, and you've made us deliciously dizzy with your whirling waltzes and the unmatched beauty of your singing voice. But we think it's time you stopped being encased exclusively in marshmallows and trifle-pudding."

As she looked around the table, Rachel could hardly speak. "I've always wanted to do a *straight* play," she finally said. "Isn't that a crazy expression, as if everything else in the theater is crooked? But frankly, gentlemen—and Mrs. Parker—I just manage to do what I'm cast in."

"Simply cast yourself upon dramatic waters," Dotty said.

"How do I do that?" Rachel wondered. "Do you think I should go to some kind of school?"

"Absolutely, " Aleck said. "And we're your faculty. Now, my lovely child. The first thing we plan to do is change your name, abbreviate it actually. Rachel Regine might be ideal for an operetta playbill, queen-like though it sounds. As you enter the larger realm of theater arts, you should call yourself simply RACHEL."

"No last name at all?"

"It's merely circumcising the superfluous," George Kaufman noted.

"But wasn't Rachel a famous French actress?"

"Not that famous, really. And she lived a century ago. Died nearly a century ago, too. And her name was pronounced Rah-shell, so there'd never be any connection. Besides, hardly anybody in America remembers her anymore. It's decided," Aleck said with total authority. "Oh. Unless you have some colossal objection."

"I don't think I do," Rachel told them with delighted confusion. "But I'm glad you've decided to let me hang on to the Rachel part. It's my real first name. Regine's not my actual last name. It never was. Mr. Romberg gave it to me when I started out in one of those road companies of *Blossom Time*. He said the Shubert brothers claimed nobody in Fargo, North Dakota would ever buy tickets to an operetta that had a singer in it with a last name like mine, let alone be able to pronounce it."

"What was the name?" F.P.A. asked, taking out some copy paper and his ever present red fountain pen.

"Rczoinszki. It's spelled R-C-Z-O-I-N-S-Z-K-I. It's Polish."

Bob Benchley observed that "Somebody oughta go to Poland and start a vowel-movement."

46

"I wasn't actually Polish. My folks were. I was born in Scranton, Pennsylvania. And the place my Papa Rczoinszki came from wasn't actually Poland. Not all the time anyway."

"I'm not exactly sure I follow that," FPA said, his notes halted midstream.

"When my father was a kid, most of the time where he lived it was the Polish part of Russia, and the rest of the time it was the Russian part of Poland."

"I think I just flunked Geography," Dotty said.

"Well, you see, the border between Russia and Poland ran practically straight through my papa's house. And it kept changing. One month they'd be in Poland and the month after that, they'd be in Russia again. My father said when he was six or seven, his papa would rush into his bedroom, wake him up, and yell: 'Favel! Great news! We're Polish again!' And he'd jump out of bed and shout: 'Thank God! I couldn't stand another Russian winter!'"

The whole Table Round hooted and hollered, and everybody declared Rachel a genius yarn-spinner, the best in the place, upstaging the lot of them. And they said that hencefoward she was a permanent member of their formerly closed society of wits and raconteurs.

They all took turns kissing Rachel on the cheek, even George Kaufman, who was known never to have kissed anybody, even his own wife. Those self-imposed restraints were destined to be lifted when, several years later, George became known as a lover of considerable facility and dimensions.

Woollcott, who usually sounded like some lightweight minnesinger, pulled out all the stops of near-profundity, his panegyric to "the new Rachel" as colorful as the wide spread of a peacock's tailfeathers.

"When we saw how you ignite a stage, with nary a spotlight needed to add to your self-created luminesence, we knew you were an instant immortal of the theater, inheriting all the golden light of the past, illuminating all the paths of the future. You already have the fervor of the great Greeks. And you have in the veins of your talent, the joy of the Commedia, passed down the years to Moliere and Sheridan, to Congreve, to the sadly brilliant Oscar Wilde, and to our new British friend, Noel Coward, all of whose ladies you will certainly play. And you will bring us infinite laughter as you mirror and make us see the follies and foibles of our own private lives.

"You will share the passion of the Passion Plays, the stained glass radiance of every chancel drama, helping to light up the world. The Mystery plays will no longer be mysteries but living prayers, and your *Everyman* will become *Everywoman*.

"We long to see you as Ophelia and all her Shakespearian sisters: Juliet, of course, and the shrew that is Kate. Cordelia perhaps, or Desdemona, and one day even Lady Macbeth, she of the blood-spotted hands. Rosalind! Portia! Calpurnia, the prototype of all the Brides of March, fearing for their husbands as does the wife of every politician in history. And Miranda, helping us to round out our own little lives with a sleep.

"You will breathe Ibsen, make love to his words and his biting conscience. Your Nora will slam doors for all the world to hear. Your Hedda will place laurel wreaths on the heads of all your admirers from Oslo to Oshkosh.

"We can't wait to taste your brimming bowl of Chekovian borscht. Just one solid boiled potato, please, and no sour cream.

"And Shaw! Lots of Shaw. Your St. Joan will convince God, who made this beautiful earth, to prepare it, at long last, to receive His saints."

All rose for a toast. The silliness of puritanical Prohibition restricted their glasses to iced tea, lemonade, a Boston Cooler (ginger ale with an ice cream float) or tomato-juice, for God's sake. But their glasses were lifted with impressiveness as if each contained vintage champagne.

"Rachel!"

"Rachel!"

"Rachel!"

"Rachel!"

"Rachel!"

"Rachel!"

"Rachel!"

"The Divine Rachel!"

And Rachel stood up and bowed, a great lady of the theater, which she already was and always would be, as long as there were audiences to applaud, to love her, to bow back to her.

X.

THE century's time clock moved ahead from 1928 through Black Monday of 1929, which affected the box office take at most theaters and the stomach-linings of most of its purveyors. They panicked when they realized that the number of Broadway productions had dipped from a happy high of 240 plays and musicals in the '28-'29 season to a Depression low of a mere 190 for '29-'30.

Variety's headline: WALL STREET LAYS AN EGG didn't cause as much terror in theater-loving heads and hearts as the gut fear that the goddam Talkies would soon reduce all stage productions to a funereal zero. They wouldn't have a platform left to pace on. Every theater in Manhattan would certainly be razed; only parking lots would be left.

But Rachel's recollections of the terminal '20s and the brink of the '30s were far less box-office statistical, far more passionately personal.

In the thoroughfares of her mind, she kept walking down the Big Street of 1930, "that hysterically historical year for me when within six months I found and lost the most important love of my life."

She told all this to Jed and Kati; well, not *all*, the how-we-met-at-the-Algonquin part of course, and about incredible moments on the stage of the Belasco, but nothing of the out-of-town tryout part in Philadelphia, which she would never talk about, not even when she talked to herself.

She had lived through the exciting but tense experience of three dramatic hits in a row, one at the Maxine Elliot Theatre, one at Henry Miller's beautiful playhouse on 43rd Street, one at the Booth. It was possible then, when a solid hit meant a long run of 100 performances, and if you had "star stuff," endurance muscles, and a damn good press agent, to perform in two or three plays in one calendar year.

As often as possible, Rachel joined the happy circumference of the Algonquin Round Table. Joshua Lewis, in a white coat with water pitcher poised, was in constant, lingering attendance, listening with all ears—at least two. She noticed him for the first time, slowing down her "I've got to rush off to rehearsal" exit when she saw Joshua; she was stopped in the shadowy exit way by the adoration in his eyes.

"You're so good looking you must be an actor," Rachel told him. "At least a movie star."

"Oh, thank you, but I'm not."

"I thought all waiters in New York were actors, or fellas who are waiters while they're waiting to be actors."

"I'm not a waiter either. Just a busboy."

And he awkwardly indicated the water pitcher in his nervously clutched fist.

"Do you like your job?"

"Not much. Bottom of the totem pole. Everybody yells at you all the time and tells you what you should do and exactly what you shouldn't do. Kicking-the-dog stuff. And the waiters you say are actors look down their noses at me. Whenever I start to ask any of 'em a question, especially the head waiter, they say: 'Shut up. You're not supposed to talk to us.'"

"Ah!" Rachel said. "You must be a writer!"

Joshua smiled, showing his handsome white teeth.

"Not really. Yet. I'm trying to be. I've started to write a play. Well, sort of a play."

"Is there a part in it for me?" Rachel asked with the instant reflex reaction of every actor who hears there's a new play somewhere, anywhere, in the wind.

"Oh, I wouldn't presume to write anything for you, Mademoiselle Rachel. "You're a big star and all the big playwrights must be lining up to write big plays for you."

"All the big playwrights don't always write big plays," she smiled. "Let me see your play when you've finished it."

"Oh, I don't think I could do that, " Joshua said with genuine humility. "I'd be afraid you wouldn't like it and I'd go right out and kill myself. It's my first play."

"Of course it is. How could you possibly be a play-wright if you never got around to writing a first play? And what would happen then to your second play, and your tenth, and your fiftieth."

"Fiftieth? Even Shakespeare only wrote thirty-seven."

"Lope de Vega wrote hundreds. Shakespeare probably slept late every morning."

They laughed mutually, as if they'd been sharing jokes for years, the surest path to intimacy.

"What's your play about?"

"About an hour long at the moment. But you make me want to go home and take the cover off my L.C. Smith typewriter and spend all night tonight and every night and try to write the second hour."

"Do you have a title?"

"*The Mandarin Lady*. It's sort of oriental."

"I've always wanted to play something like Cio-Cio-San in *Madame Butterfly*, but I was always more operetta in my strictly musical days than I was opera. Did you know, incidentally, that Mr. Puccini based that on a play written by Mr. Belasco down the street?"

"That's Japanese. Mine is more Chinese actually."

"How'd a nice American boy like you happen to write about China?"

"After I finished college, I went and lived there for a year. I got on a tramp steamer and then on a junk up the Yangstze and just settled in for awhile. A lot of time to think. A lot of rice. A lot of learning how to respect older people."

"Where was college?"

"Oberlin. In Ohio."

She glanced at her watch.

"I'm sorry," he apologized. "You're going to be late for rehearsal."

"Don't *you* be late sending me your play. The minute it's finished."

With a helpless impulse, she leaned forward and kissed Joshua on the cheek. Then she dashed off to her rehearsal at the Lyceum.

XI

Six weeks later, Rachel remembered, Joshua handed her a playscript in the lobby of the Algonquin. Then he turned and raced through the Rose Room into its back-stage area, the kitchen. A long time afterwards she found out that he had averaged three and a half hours sleep a night in his one-room coldwater flat so he could finish his play. For her.

She read *The Mandarin Lady* that night in her slightly larger quarters at the Hotel, not quite a suite but almost, marveling at the play's poetry, its warmth, its capture of the Oriental Tao of living. And she knew that every page Joshua had written was an act of love.

The leading role was a part any actress might cherish: a beautiful Chinese maiden in Act I, a caring middle-aged matriarch in Act II, and a philosophic nonagenarian in Act III. But when she flipped the manuscript pages back to the cast list, she shook her head and asked herself a ques-tion out loud: "These days what producer would ever put this on the stage? Thirty actors! And almost the same number of sets!"

When she saw Joshua next, on the street in front of the hotel, all she could look at was the questioning, hopeful, tell-me-it-isn't-terrible look in his eyes.

"It's wonderful, Joshua," she said, but she kept walk-ing up 44th Street toward Broadway, talking to him over her shoulder. "It's a beautiful play. And I'm going to do something about it. I'm not exactly sure what, but something."

She thought she'd by-pass agents, knowing they would take months to read a play. They would certainly shove it to the bottom of an endless stack of unread scripts, especially one by an unknown playwright. She didn't dare ask for a second opinion or the use of influence by her confreres on the Table Round: a rejection by even a single member of the mighties of New York's Rivoli would be a wound beyond healing for the super-sensitive Joshua.

Rachel wrote a note to the Theatre Guild, asking if they might be interested in a play she had in hand, telling of her own availability at the moment to star in it. Her current producers had cancelled the announced-in-the-columns work in mid-rehearsal, failing to tell the cast or anybody that they had lost all their backing in the stock market crash. (She didn't state in the letter that Equity and the Dramatists Guild were suing, but found no one left around to sue.) Theresa Helburn of the Theatre Guild wrote back a polite note saying frankly that they had scheduled Shaw and O'Neill for this and next season and couldn't possibly consider any other new plays. But they admired her work and hoped Rachel would be on the Guild stage some day in the very near future. They were contemplating a new Molnar play for the '32-'33 season: would she be willing to come in and read for them?

"No, I wouldn't," Rachel said aloud, and tossed the letter into an Algonk (as she began to call it) wastebasket.

She went in person to see George Abbott, who flipped through pages, saying with a grim faced smile that it didn't seem to be his cup of tea, but would Rachel like to go dancing some night soon?

"Not my glass of tea," Max Gordon said, scanning the

script as he sat at his messy desk beneath a second story plate glass window that couldn't possibly have been washed for twenty years. "My God in holy heaven!" he continued as he turned back to the cast page. "A play like this would cost eighteen maybe twenty thousand dollars. Who's got money like that? Sam Harris and I swore on our mothers' graves we'd never put on a play that cost more than ten thousand bucks, not ever. Maybe twelve thousand five if it's got George Kaufman's name on it, but not a dime more. I gotta be frank with you, sweetheart, with prices going up and the Dramatists Guild, George too, shoving their cockamamie minimum contract down our throats, I may have to go out of business altogether."

Rachel shrugged her thanks, took back the play manuscript, and started out of the office. Max ran after her, stopping her at the head of the stairs.

"You're a nice girl. I like you. Good actress. I go to all opening nights. Yours too, so I know. Lemme give you a hint. There's a young fella name of Sanderson from a filthy rich Long Island family who's been hokking-my-chainik he's gotta be a producer, damn fool. And I got a hunch he wants to do plays like this one looks like, even arty-shmartier than the Theatre Guild. And he's got the cash money, not from his father, but from the number one bootlegger, the one who gets all the rum-running booze for the speak-easies, 21 and Tony's, a lot of 'em, which has gotta make him the richest man in New York, John D. Rockefeller included. So maybe he's the only one left in town who can afford to bankroll theater anymore. Come back in the office, I'll give you the Sanderson kid's phone number. I'm only doin' this 'cause I want to see you on a stage again. Quick."

Jerome Sanderson, the potential producer, came for tea with Rachel in the Algonquin lobby. Joshua was along,

56

shed of his busboy's white coat, wearing an old school necktie and a corduroy jacket with leather patches at the elbows. Jerry Sanderson wore a blue blazer and white flannel trousers; a tennis racket seemed to be seriously missing.

"Miss Rachel was good enough to send me your play, Mr. Lewis, and I want to tell you that, in my opinion, this has to win the Pulitzer Prize. If it doesn't, I'm going to demand that Yale send back all the tuition money my father paid them. So naturally, I want to produce your play."

Rachel squeezed Joshua's hand under the table. He was too excited to say anything to either of them, and his teacup started to rattle.

"I hope you won't mind if my major backer, Joey Massi, gets co-producer billing. You may know his work: he's in the beverage business. He wants very much to be part of the cultural scene, which I find commendable."

Joshua didn't mind anything, only that his play was heading for Broadway, only that the Divine Rachel would be its star.

Luise Sillcox at the Dramatists Guild, then in four small rooms and a long corridor at 6 E. 39th, was delighted that their former part-time file clerk, now a full fledged member, had insisted on the Minimum Basic Agreement for his play. Joshua actually got a $500 advance against royalties and a guarantee of per diem when his play went out of town for a tryout. The busboy-file clerk was en route to immortality.

XII.

ALL eight New York daily newspapers printed the public declaration by the fabled David Belasco that he had
decided to "cease the sordid, overwhelming paper work,
the tin cup in hand beggary of raising money which
plagued every working theater manager." The *New York
World* even ran it on their front page, with a two column
head and a photograph, complete with a priestly reverse
collar, of "The Jewish Bishop of Broadway."

Young would-be producer Jerome Sanderson rushed to
take Belasco up on his amended statement that the great
man might still "rent my beautiful theater on West 44th
Street to a fellow-artist, provided I approve of the
playscript, still have some creative supervision of the new
work, and perhaps even, if persuaded, direct the play."

"Belasco! Belasco! Belasco! Perfect!" Sanderson shouted to Rachel and Joshua, startling the rest of the customers in the crowded Sardi's. "The Belasco Theatre!
Perfect for this play. The director perfect, too. Everything
perfect. The star! The play! Playwright, are you happy?"

"I think I'd have been happy if a few actors had read
my play aloud in a church basement," Joshua said. "But
sure I'm happy. Who wouldn't be?"

At the Midtown Mimeograph Shop, ink-stained hands
handled sticky blue stencils to turn out forty copies of the
playscript. The legendary Belasco didn't wait for signed

contracts to begin his customary rituals for a new play, even before he met the dramatist or the star. He dispatched troops of helpers to the households of New York's Chinatown to gather authentic props and set pieces down to chopsticks and cooking utensils, insisting they not be American-made or copied but sworn-to-Buddah brought or imported from the depths of China. Everybody suspected that the 71 year old Belasco had the precognition that this might be his last fling at directing in his own sacred shrine or anywhere (in fact, he died a year later, in 1931) so he was trying to duplicate his celebrated passion for realism. In 1909, for *The Easiest Way,* he had bought and put on stage an entire floor of an 8th Avenue boarding house, insisting it be from 8th Avenue and nowhere else, because that's what the playwright had written. And in 1912, for *The Governor's Lady,* he perfectly matched on stage a Childs Restaurant, spoon for spoon.

How would all this work for Joshua's somewhat poetic and ethereal play? Only God and Belasco knew. Joshua and Rachel were comforted with the knowledge that Giacomo Puccini had fashioned a masterwork out of Belasco's original play, *Madame Butterfly* after seeing it in London, literal staging no matter. Even though the subsequent opera flopped amid hoots and boos when it premiered at Milan's La Scala in 1904, its soaring melodies had since become immortal. Perhaps a touch of the literal might keep Joshua's theater-feet on the ground. Or maybe star, dramatist, and nouveau-producer were kidding themselves. For it wasn't just a touch.

To attend the first called rehearsal, Rachel insisted on walking the short block from the "Algonk" to the stage door of the Belasco on the playwright's arm. The stage doorman took off his cap, bowed to Rachel in a courtly manner, and handed her a dressing room key marked #I, emblazoned with a star. Then, with a graceful sweep of his arm, unlike any stage doorman she'd ever seen, he indicated the direction through the fire door toward the stage.

Joshua, slightly terrified, lingered in the wings. Rachel patted his hand, trying to calm the racing pulse in his wrist. Then she turned, puzzled to find a maze of props and preliminary pieces of primitive Oriental furniture already on stage. Dead center a worklight, a bare bulb in an iron cage, sent out faint beams, a dwarfed lighthouse in a sea of clutter. Twenty nine other actors were already searching for props labeled in large letters the part assigned to each of them and, in far smaller letters, their names. Rachel recognized some of the actors and longtime Belasco associates, others were new to her. When they saw her, they set down their props or placed them under their arms, and applauded her. She graciously nodded her thanks, her eyes squinting in the half light for a first glimpse of the mighty Belasco. He was apparently waiting to make an entrance. A property master appeared from the wings, almost obsequiously handed Rachel a blue Chinese bowl of steaming rice, two ornamented chopsticks dug into one side.

Suddenly a pin-spot focused on Row C, seat #117, down front center of the audience side of the theater. An unseen figure came down the right aisle and crossed to the lighted seat, but remained standing, drinking in the light. Rachel was startled by her first in-person look at the man she had only seen before in photographs. A shock of silvery-white hair, curled over his broad forehead above jet-black eyebrows, made him seem taller, more imposing than his five-feet-six height. His brown eyes were penetrating and he wore a priest's turned around collar, with a tiny v-vent in front, pointing upward toward his throat.

Though his voice was deep, it had the eager enthusiasm of a small boy about to play for the first time with a new toy.

"Ladies and gentlemen, I am David Belasco."

Again applause from all the actors. Rachel looked about quickly to find a place to put down her bowl of rice. Knowing she couldn't tuck it under her arm, she compensated for failing to applaud with a respectful bow, making certain not to spill a grain of hot rice.

"I welcome you to my theater. No, I humbly beg your pardon. I welcome you now, for the entire rehearsal period, and for the run of this play, to the tiny village of Shan-Tzu in the Province of Honan. For that microcosm amidst the great land mass, which is the ancient country of China, is no longer nine thousand miles away but here, on this stage."

Everyone in the cast held up a prop, or clutched it more tightly. Rachel looked around then quickly fell into the mood by expertly manipulating her chopsticks and deftly eating a blob of rice.

"You are an actress of my stripe, my dear Rachel," Belasco intoned. "Though some nouveau critics have castigated me for what they call my over-meticulousness, I do not see it as such. We are creating reality beyond reality. Every member of the audience will feel that each of them is holding a rice bowl as you are doing, and tasting each grain as you taste it. Here! My loyal stagehands! Move the bed-of-straw downstage center."

The obedient backstage crew hurried on-stage and shoved the wooden cot into place as directed.

"We will not boast of our creative empathy with a program note saying that this crude bed once sat on the dirt floor of a peasant's shack in the actual Province of Honan. But *I* will be aware of this truth as I direct, and you,

Rachel, will know this truth when you climb into your
wedding night bed to receive your husband's masculinity
as he embraces your loveliness. And the audience will
know, too. Every watching woman will feel it is *her* wedding night. And each man in this theater will be paying
tribute to you, sensing it is *he* who is instilling a brand-new
life into your beautiful body."

Rachel, impressed, touched the straw on the bed. The
great Belasco turned businesslike, calling out. "Playwriter! Do we have a playwriter here?"

Joshua timidly appeared at the edge of the proscenium,
awkwardly half-raised a hand as if asking a 3rd grade
schoolteacher for permission to go to the little-boys' room.

"Good. You notice I do not call you a playwright,
spelled p-l-a-y-w-r-i-g-h-t, in the popular fashion, as if you
were akin to a wheelwright. Oh, I agree that every play
should be like a smoothly-moving cart, with no wheels
with flat-bottoms which would make it bump along. But,
though I respect craft, we playwriters must be more than
mere mechanics. We are artists! I speak, with no modesty
whatsoever, from experience: I have written or collabo-
rated on the writing of more than two hundred plays, most
of them presented on this stage."

He reached an outstretched hand toward the steps
from the stage into the audience, gesturing for Joshua to
join him.

"Come. Sit here beside me, boy. But no talk. No interruptions." He turned to his actors. "From anyone! All I
wish to hear in this Temple of Truth are the living sounds
of the beautiful words written by young Mister—what was
your name again?"

"Joshua Lewis."

"— whose truths shall shatter walls like Jericho, whose
imagination will echo all the way to the village of Shan-

Tzu and, indeed, transport that ancient village to this stage."

Joshua quietly moved to seat #119 in Row C, reverent as Joshua of old, staring up at Moses handing down the Commandments on tablets of stone.

"As a fellow playwriter of this boy-Joshua, I almost religiously respect his vision," Belasco said softly, then he thundered at his cast. "So I shall demand that you change not a single word, not a syllable, not a punctuation mark. No improvisations, please. No needless additions or subtractions. No distorting rearrangement of sentences. Unless *I* tell you to."

XIII

Every day of rehearsal the cast was engulfed in newly arrived Chinese props, set pieces, stage machinery rising from the depths of the stage, lifting a mountain peak so that the top of it soared toward the flies. Belasco announced with fitting pride that bushels of red earth, now tucked into the holds of freighters, would be arriving from Honan Province by the time they reached the mountain-climbing climax of Act III. The winding paths leading to the plateaus or way-stops of their stage mountain would be packed with genuine soil from the hillsides of China.

Rachel knew that Belasco's insistence on scenic flamboyance could not be challenged: it was his artistic trademark, notably when he'd shipped a ton of earth from the gold mining gulches of California to stack on stage for *The Girl of the Golden West*. But something in her star lady bloodstream made her realize that the scenery of *The Mandarin Lady* was rapidly becoming its star. For the first time during the rehearsal process, she spoke back to the priestly director.

"Is all this really necessary? It seems to me, as I study the play, that the end of Act III is fantasy, pure imagination inside the head of the climber. The young writer hears disembodied voices in his search for truth. As he climbs the paths toward the mountain top, he doesn't absorb all this through his sandals, through his big toes."

An insincere smile masked Belasco's indignation at being challenged. "The reality makes the imagination more imaginative. You, as a great actress, must realize that. The truth, the actual truth of everything around us, sets all our imaginations free."

Then he turned his back on her.

"But doesn't all this cost a lot of money? Don't the producers object?"

Belasco wheeled around. "If all you are concerned about is money, you stop being an artist. Go. Rush off to the money factories of Hollywood. They'll pour liquid gold over you, turn you into a mercenary goddess."

He waved toward the head of the aisles, then toward the stage door.

"As for the producers, I have directed my goodly and loyal front-of-the house minions, as well as the veteran guardian of my stage door, never to admit those bastards to this chapel of creativity while we are in the process of shaping a masterpiece. They are to attend no rehearsals. We might possibly admit them, briefly, for a run-through when we are ready, when we *say* we are ready. Meanwhile, I shall countenance no interference from some Yale-pretentious playboy. Nor shall I allow a bootlegger, masquerading as a mavin of culture, to breathe his foul and drunken breath on my beautiful and delicate play."

Quickly, Belasco corrected himself. "On *Joshua's* beautiful play. I apologize to you, my dear boy. I am not the creator of this work, possibly, briefly, during this rehearsal process, I might be considered a co-creator. Never a god. You might think I'm pretending to be Zeus-on-high when we have our first run-through. For I shall be watching from a peephole atop the second balcony. But I'll never fling lightning bolts down upon players or playwriter. I'll be there merely as a messenger of the gods, watching from the heights of Olympus as it were, to make certain there is divine beauty in the total stage picture, and that I can hear the clear and resonant reach of your voices. And the voice of the play itself."

On other days, he indulged in less theatrical philosophizing but more Belascovian backstage peccadilloes. One female member of the cast, playing a middle-aged woman of the village, had one moment of shouted warning, another of whispered gossip. To the despair of the director, she could never play either moment with dramatic effectiveness. After several attempts to coach the recalcitrant actress, Belasco turned sternly to Rachel, his voice raised so the entire cast could hear.

"You call yourself an actress? Don't you realize who the most important person is on the living stage? The speaker? No! The listener! The watcher! But you are listening and watching all wrong! When this talented actress so cunningly whispers the delicious gossip of the village into your ear, your face has the emotion of a sheet of blank paper. And later when she rushes through the door of your shack, shattering the air with her scream of terror, I am chilled to the bone. But you react as if you never even heard her, or saw her come in the room, though the marvel of her shout is the climactic moment of the play."

Belasco turned from the puzzled Rachel to the other actress. "Shall we try those moments once again—for the benefit of our naughty star?"

"May I have a minute or two to get into it, to commune with myself?"

"But of course, dear."

The middle-aged actress disappeared momentarily into the wings. Belasco quickly pulled Rachel aside, with a smiling whisper. "My apologies. That wasn't for you at all. You've been perfect. It was entirely for *her* benefit."

But when she returned to the stage, the moments were still misplayed; Belasco's ploy or her communion with herself had benefited her not a bit. This time the director directed her directly.

"You are whispering when you should shout and shouting when you should whisper. What in the name of sweet God do you think you're doing?"

"I don't understand that at all. I don't feel—inside—that I'm doing that. I think Mr. Belasco is wrong."

Now an enraged Belasco shouted at her.

"You don't understand Belasco! You think Belasco is wrong, do you? I don't give a shit what you're feeling. I want what *I'm* feeling and what I'm hearing or not hearing. I want the *audience* to do the feeling!"

And he fumbled at the front of his vest, furiously unsnapping a large pocket watch from a golden chain. Dramatically he lifted the watch, apparently of pure gold, above his head, then, with full force, smashed it to the stage floor. Everybody gasped. The middle-aged actress screamed as she should have screamed in the lamented moment of the play.

"Now see what you've made Belasco do? This is the most precious heirloom of my life, left to me by my sainted grandfather. Do you have any *feeling* now that I've smashed the greatest treasure I've ever owned? It's your fault, your *un*feeling behavior, your not listening to Belasco, which has caused this tragedy. Rehearsal is dismissed."

Weeping, the middle-aged actress ran into the wings, and out the stage door. Belasco pulled Rachel away from her fixed stare at the pieces of broken glass and watch casing, the twisted springs, the little metal wheels and scattered screws. He winked at her slyly.

"Come. Climb with me to my office. I want to show you

something. And you'll have an opportunity to look down on this disaster from my peephole high on Olympus."

Belasco escorted Rachel into his office-apartment-museum with a sweep of his hand at the treasures on the mahogany shelves, at framed mementos papering the walls, mostly Napoleonic artifacts, original letters and decrees in the flourishing French handwriting of Bonaparte himself. How appropriate this was, Rachel thought, as she stared at her director, who stood at the dead center of his aerie with the brooding arrogance of that half mad, self-appointed Emperor.

The man in the turned-around collar suddenly did a comic turn from his imperial pose to elfin-like playfulness as he almost danced with delight toward an armoire. He winked at Rachel again, putting a finger to his lips to indicate that this was to be their private secret. He lifted out a large wooden box, opened its lid, and gleefully showed Rachel twenty or more watches, identical to the smashed one on the stage floor. And he laughed with great delight.

"That actress with delusions of adequacy will do those scenes perfectly tomorrow. You'll see. This always works—but I can only do it once per play."

Then he led Rachel to his peephole, inviting her to "look down there." As she did, she felt she was somewhere in outer space, standing on the moon perhaps, with a distant view of the tiny picture frame which was the planet-stage. Light years away, far below, stagehands were sweeping up the tin and glass crumbs of Belasco's smashed mock-golden watch.

XIV.

THE day of the first scheduled run-through, Belasco reluctantly allowed the two previously frustrated producers to sit in the back row of the orchestra. "But no other shlep-along guests," he ordered. "And no interruptions whatsoever."

From his guardian angel-like perch behind his peep-hole, Belasco failed to notice an academic looking gentleman with a Vandycke beard who managed to slip by and sit beside the producers beneath the cover of the protruding balconies. He turned out to be a drama professor from Yale, recruited by his one-time student, newborn producer Jerome Sanderson, for "expert advice."

Nor did Belasco see the the trio storm out of the theater, after a tense, totally silent deathwatch through all three acts, and head west on 44th Street toward Times Square. They had hired the best suite at the Astor, and waited for the star and dramatist to show up for their simmering advice.

When they arrived, the Professor, whose name Rachel managed to forget immediately and for all time, kissed her hand. "You are a brilliant actress. We of the world of theater scholarship consider you a national treasure. If you were a star of the English stage, you would be on the verge of being declared a Dame-of-the-Order-of-the-British-Empire. But!"

Everybody waited for the scholar to finish his sentence. Joshua closed his eyes.

"Even your performing genius, my dear lady, cannot surmount David Belasco's production. It is a tedious disaster."

Rachel indignantly rose to her feet.

"You're wrong. I love this play. I love this young man's words."

"I might be persuaded to agree with you. If I could hear the words. But most of them have been buried under piles of Chinese dirt. In my scholarly opinion, Mr. Belasco belongs in the old fasioned hell of scenic cliches along with mountings of the works of Dion Boucicault and that entire bunch of theatrical anachronisms. This play is poetry, not an exacting lunch at Childs Restaurant. It needs the soaring imagination of Robert Edmond Jones or Lee Simonson or that young Jo Mielziner, or perhaps no scenery at all. Lights only. A few platforms. Space. Air. A symbolic monolith in the manner of Adolphe Appia. Too bad he died just two years ago or you could have brought him over from Switzerland."

Jerome Sanderson seemed devastated, especially when he glanced at his co-producer and major backer, whose expression made it seem he was about to toss his cookies, bad public relations for a mogul of the beverage business.

"What's your feeling, Joey?" Sanderson asked solicitously.

"I gotta be frank with you. I ain't no teach like the Professor here, but me, I go to a show to have a good time. Like for instance when I see Flo Ziegfeld's *Follies*—he's a good customer of mine and he always delivers the goods the same way I do. Girls. Beautiful girls. Lots of 'em. I look at a show like that and I want to sleep with everybody in the place—not the fellas, of course—but all the dames, not throwin' the cute lady ushers outa bed. Nobody in this Mandarin thing I'd go across the street to cop a good feel. Except, of course, you, Dame Rachel."

"Thank you very much," Rachel said icily, not considering it a compliment.

"I'm sorry," Joshua said quietly. "I'm sorry about the whole thing." And he started to leave the Astor suite.

"Wait!" the Professor said, fingering his beard. "I think the work can be saved. A brilliant director, a man who's worked with Reinhardt in Salzburg and Vakhtangov in Moscow, is now in residence at Yale: Ludwig Kronheim. He feels as I do about the theater and I think he could be convinced to take over the direction of your play."

"Can we do that? Can we kick Belasco out of his own theater?"

"We've got nothing in writing but the lease of the four walls, box office stop clauses and all that," young Sanderson said, the self-made Broadway expert, having religiously read *Variety* for a full year and confident he was speaking the lingo like an old-timer. "All Belasco owns is the theater. We own the play, as long as we stay kosher with the author. And after we get back from two weeks at the Forrest in Philly, if Belasco wants to cancel our booking, fine and dandy, that's his funeral, nothing else is coming in. Lot of Shubert houses going begging, including the Cort, the National, the Longacre, lot of others. The Shuberts'll grab us, especially with Rachel here above the title."

"What's *your* feeling about David Belasco?" the Professor asked Rachel. "Personally. And as an actress."

Rachel took a stand, solid on her feet as Portia.

"He's a lovable, terrible, wonderful, sometimes brilliant, sometimes stupid genius who can be an awful pain-in-the-ass. Is that scholarly enough for you, Professor?"

"From now on all pain stops," Sanderson said. "Tomorrow morning, we're gonna hire Ludwig Kronheim."

XV.

THE tall, imposing Ludwig Kronheim, with a thick Austrian accent, took command of the little emperor's battlefield, banished the scenery clutter to the Elba of the flats of New Jersey, and exiled the silent Belasco to his own St. Helena behind the theater's upper balcony.

Joshua was appalled at the terrible waste of burning discarded sets, but that seemed to be the standing order of procedure with the commercial theater. He was not unhappy with the simple platforms and lighting plot which evolved: his imaginative words were allowed to paint the scenery.

With the exception of Rachel, the roles began to be recast, one by one. "These are meant to be simple villagers," Kronheim intoned. "These characters have been posturing impossibly as if they are flamboyant noblemen or royalty, yet with no sense of the majesty of the language, and no awareness of the universality of its very simplicity."

Rachel felt Kronheim was only talking for the sake of talking; his perpetual lectures on mitteleuropean dramatic theories made her want to say "horseshit", but she only said it to herself. When each member of the original cast, except Rachel, became "at liberty", she winced at this expression for the kind of "freedom" no actor ever wanted.

Rachel pulled Kronheim aside to plead for gentleness in this mass dismissal. "Tell them that there have been rewrites, that each of them was perfect, absolutely perfect before, when it was a totally different concept of the play."

"Liebchen," Kronheim said, "you are teaching your grandmother how to suck eggs."

Rehearsals were extended two weeks so that the Austrian Master could "grapple with the subtext and simultaneously lessen the needless operatic grandeur of the production into its needed tone: the simplicity of a Chinese lullaby."

Rachel didn't disagree with the shedding of scenery, feeling more unfettered in her performance. But with every change and cut in the text her mind bled a little, knowing Joshua was having daily hemorrhages. She comforted him, holding his hand, repeating George Abbott's oft-quoted advice to playwrights: "Sure, you have to make changes. But be damn sure every change is a change for the better. Because it's just as easy to make changes for the worse." She felt many Kronheim-imposed rewrites were changes for the worse, but she didn't tell Joshua that. And she often fought for a line or a particular page of dialogue when she felt it was worth fighting for.

After one rehearsal, with only two days until their move to Philadelphia, Rachel asked for a moment alone on the Belasco stage. When the others had left, the work light her only companion, she came to the lip of the platform and stared up at the closed peephole above the balconies.

Quietly, not sure he was even listening or watching, she half spoke, half sang a bittersweet hymn of praise.

"Dear Mr. Belasco. Dear David, which I have never dared to call you. You are the sweet psalm singer of the living stage. And we don't want to leave you, or have you leave us. Ever. In many ways, I love you. For you love what I love: the theater and the life of the theater. I love you for your laughter: when you laugh at our foolishness and sometimes even at your own. I love you for your anger: when you're angry at the right things. I applaud your search for truth, but all of us too often bury our new found truths in lies, as our playwriter has written so eloquently. But I thank you for what I have learned from you. It isn't easy to learn, for we must first unlearn shabby old habits and flush away a lot of egotistical certainties. In short, dear David, you have sandpapered our souls."

* * *

Philadelphia rarely remains the City of Brotherly Love when a Broadway-bound show is "in trouble out of town." The beautiful Forrest Theater was a constant joy with one exception: the un-stage-wise architect had failed to include dressing rooms or even backstage toilets, which made one wag comment that the behind-the-curtain area "was positively un-canny." The hastily built addition had to be constructed with an alley separating it from the stage, for God-knows what kind of municipal fire ordinances. Actors then and to this day are forced to cross from their dressing-rooms to the the theater either beneath the alley, steps down, steps up again, or through often blustery weather via the shorter route through the open alley. Wintertime booked plays, with costumes and wigs buffeted in the breeze, seem on occasion to resemble *King Lear.*

When sunshine was beaming down on play and players, out of town tryouts often turned into games of sexual musical-chairs. In the case of *The Mandarin Lady*, nobody had time or energy left to play that extra-curricular game.

The cast was spread across the city in a variety of hotels: The Warwick, the old Bellevue-Stratford, and the stately Barclay, where Rachel stayed, with a fine view from her suite down onto Rittenhouse Square. Joshua bunked at the Y.M.C.A., saving most of his per diem for later months, in the dread prospect that future royalties might cease in the event of an instant Broadway flop.

Rachel found a way to "comfort him with apples," not only from the fruit bowl sent up to the star by the Barclay management, but with warmth and affection and genuine encouragement.

For nobody in Philadelphia tossed his hat in the air for Joshua's play. The opening night audience shrugged its approval, applauded its star, didn't like the work very much, or really understood it. The reviews seemed vaguely hopeful but not very helpful. The cynical press agent, searching for quotes for Sunday ads in the *Bulletin* and the *Inquirer*, could only come up with two self-composed lines of not very amusing satire: "*The Mandarin Lady* was met with a wave of militant indifference" and "Nearly everybody in Philadelphia hates this play." The quotes finally printed were praise for Rachel, but no cheers for play or playwright.

Jerome Sanderson, whose fellow-producer remained bottled up in Manhattan when no dancing dames had been added to the production, pontificated in *Variety*-ese that "people are staying away from the B.O. in droves due to the non-money notices and the fact that Wall Street laid an egg, which means that the play needs work, in fact major rewrites."

Every night Joshua stayed up from curtain fall to nearly dawn in a top floor dressing room at the theater-annex, pounding out pages of rewrites, reworking, polishing, clarifying, numbing his senses with lack of sleep. An assistant stage manager would arrive at sunup to rush pages to mimeograph, preparing for the painful rehearsals, ll:00 A.M. to 4:00 P.M. except matinee days. After a hasty read through of the new material, Kronheim would invariably toss the script pages aside and say: "It's getting there, but it hasn't quite got the essence, the flavor, the *gestalt* I want. Each of you improvise this scene in tonight's performance in the tone I have directed you, and we'll see how it works." It never did, except when Rachel went back to the original text syllable for syllable.

Joshua tried to conquer the confining claustrophobia of the late at night, stale air dressing room by regular walks around the wooded block of Rittenhouse Square. He hoped the fresh air would bring him fresh ideas. And he composed a little song in his head as he tried to inhale deep breaths of inspiration:

> I used to think all plays were play,
> But then I threw my toys away.
> To get my talent out of hock,
> I walked around my writing-block:
> When I was written out in Rittenhouse Square.

One parading-around-the-block time, long past midnight, he glanced high up on the façade of The Barclay and saw lights still burning in the windows of Rachel's suite. Despite frowns from the doorman and the disapproval of the night clerk at the way-down-the-corridor front desk, Joshua was announced and invited up.

Rachel came to the door. She wore a negligee and had a nearly empty champagne glass in her hand.

"Come in, come in, dear Joshua. I hate drinking champagne alone, so I'm glad you're here. The first bottle is almost gone, but look! There are two, in case of some dire emergency like a beautiful young man showing up."

"I'm a bastard for busting in like this in the middle of the night. You've got a matinee tomorrow and you'll miss your beauty sleep."

"I never consider that a compliment. It's as if the complimenter is saying: 'Hey, lady, you're not really very beautiful, you have to sleep your way into it.'"

Joshua smiled an "I didn't mean that" smile, enjoying the bubbling of her champagne-induced humor. He opened the second bottle which had been chilling itself in a silver Barclay bucket. He poured into both glasses, they toasted silently, then she kissed him on the lips.

"My!" she said, eyes very close to eyes. "You're even better looking with worry wrinkles. I know a sure cure for them, though I'm not so sure I want them cured, just to go away for a while." Slightly tipsy, playfully devilish, she whispered into his ear: "Let's have a matinee."

"A performance of the play? A run-through? Now? Right here? I know all the lines, all the original lines anyhow. I'd be glad to cue you."

"No! No! I mean a performance of us. You dear, sweet, innocent boy, don't you know what 'Let's have a matinee' means? She's so in love with him, and he with her, that they can't wait, so they have love in the afternoon. Not just kiss-kiss love, but the whole distance. Make love in broad daylight, or love to a broad in daylight, take your choice," she added, tempering her suddenly guilty forwardness with a lame joke. "But we can rewrite that scene, turn noon into midnight and have that matinee right now."

Rachel and Joshua made love all night, warm in each other's arms. Only one moment seemed to her like an intermission, or an "interval" as the Brits would call it.

"What's the matter? What's wrong? What are you thinking about?"

"You."

"No you're not. Your mind seems far, far away. I know what it is. You're thinking of your third act, which you shouldn't do when you and I are still in the middle of the first act."

Hurt, he started to get out of bed. She pulled him back, kissing his eyes, cradling his head.

"Oh, damn! I sound like a critic. I didn't mean to. You make lovely love. I give you four stars. Raves. You're a hit. I want you to run forever!"

The smiling Joshua watched the light of dawn streaming over the treetops of Rittenhouse Square.

"Is it all right to keep having a nighttime matinee in the morning?" he asked her.

"It's the best time, you darling boy. Besides, matinee means morning, in French of course. And in church language, matins means morning prayers. I have to confess I haven't been praying, but I have had a religious experience."

Their loving laughter-filled matinee continued until it was almost time to rush to the Forrest to make half-hour call for her onstage matinee. She gave a glowing performance.

XVI

OPENING night at the Belasco in New York was a disaster. Joshua, in a rented tux, paced nervously on the worn red carpet at the back of the theater. One critic fell asleep halfway through the first act, and his loud snore made the rest of the audience break into laughter at the most touching moment of the play. Two other critics walked out after the first act. Joshua hid in the men's room and threw up.

Eight daily newspapers in Manhattan in 1930 included not merely the *New York Times*, but the *Herald-Tribune* and two other morning papers, and four in the afternoon. "Money notices" impelled people to spend their money at the box office, even during a Depression. Not a single review of *The Mandarin Lady* sold a single ticket.

Woollcott, Rachel's mentor, was expected to arrive in style at the opening, and to "toss his hat in the air" for the play on his popular radio broadcast, "The Town Crier." He had long ceased being a daily critic, either on the *Times* or the *New York World*. The current highly respected critic on the *Times*, J. Brooks Atkinson, also a Rachel-aficionado, was certain to recognize and applaud in print her sensitive performance and the high literary quality of the work itself.

But Woollcott had undoubtedly heard theater gossip out of Philadelphia, which regularly arrived in Manhattan faster than the express trains. Not wanting to commit insincere flattery, he wired his regrets, apologizing that he was confined to his trundle bed on his remote island, "Wit's End," with a combination of asthma and overeating. Atkinson's review, all two paragraphs of it, was in the midnight edition, snatched from the loading platform of the *Times*, which rubbed shoulders with Sardi's, where Atkinson's fulsome praise was scheduled to be read aloud at the opening night party. Nobody came to the party, not the star, not the suddenly-vanished playwright, not Kronheim, not the producers.

Everybody read Atkinson's shrugging review at breakfast the next morning. It was kind to Rachel, "America's most glowing actress," but questioned how she was trapped into a play "which was pseudo-Chinese, rescued from Mr. Belasco's usual chop suey, but turned into a foreign fiasco, whose attempted poetry has been served up as Mitteleuropian goulash." He further advised, as a former book critic, that his readers would do better to stay at home and read more authentic China lore, Pearl Buck's current best seller, *The Good Earth*.

It was Columnist Walter Winchell in the morning *New York Mirror* who administered the coup de grâce and made Joshua Lewis a Man Without a Play. Top of his column, Winchell wrote: "Broadway's beauty, the Divine Rachel, trod the boards of the Belasco last night in *The Mandarin Lady*. That was no lady, kiddos, that was a stinkeroo. Why she let them turn her into a hag in Act III is anybody's guess. Rumor hath it that during the Philly tryout (they didn't try hard enough) Rachel and her boy-playwright have been closerthanthis. They shoulda stood in bed instead of putting us all to sleep at the Belasco."

That did it for the jumpy producers. They didn't wait for the "hints of greatness" review from John Mason

Brown in the afternoon *Post* or hopeful forthcoming magazine pieces by Benchley in *New Yorker* (who wrote: "It
ain't *Abie's Irish Rose* but I liked it") or the month-away-
praise from George Jean Nathan in *Vanity Fair*, who
declared: "Forgive me, Brooks, me no likee *The Good
Earth*, me likee *The Mandarin Lady*, play and player."

The producers posted the closing notice. Even the simple platforms and the Appia-like Chinese monolith would
be consigned to the flames on the Jersey flats as early as
possible the following Monday morning.

Rachel wept, not because this was, in the unfortunate
terminology of the Big Street, "her first flop," but because
of her fury at the vulgar invasion of her privacy. She
screamed that we were turning into a nation of keyhole-
watchers, not by the puritanical moralists but by the gossip
mongering tabloids, who had no constitutional right to
watch her anyplace except on a stage. Her memory of that
all night matinee in Philadelphia would live with her, and
no Winchell or his ilk could force her to deny it or forget it.

Rachel's tears were primarily because she felt she had
lost Joshua, that she would never see him again. Nobody
could find him. The front-of-the-house attendants at the
Belasco reported that he had raced down 44th Street a
moment after final curtain, even beating the remaining
opening night critics out of the theater. As he almost vio-
lently ripped off his tuxedo black tie, he seemed, they
said, to be running with his eyes closed, dashing toward
nowhere.

The Belasco stage doorman recalled that the playwright had appeared backstage briefly during the third act
of the final performance on Saturday night. He watched
from the darkness of the wings for a few minutes until all
the actors were on stage, then went from dressing room to
dressing room, Rachel's included, gathering up play-

scripts. Even the production stage manager had his script grabbed from under his nose during curtain calls. Without a word, Joshua dumped all of the copies of his play into a large bag and, not turning back, went out the stage door, slamming it behind him.

The basement mimeograph shop also gave the producers a strange report: Joshua had appeared frantically the day the first reviews came out, stormed in, and ripped up the ink stained blue mimeograph stencils of his play.

"You can't do that," they protested. "Those belong to us—and to the producers, who paid for them."

"Not any more they don't," Joshua yelled, as he ran out, depositing the whole mess of ripped up stencils into the nearest garbage pail.

And Joshua waved a bitter good-bye to the mimeograph ladies and to Broadway, with ink stained hands.

XVII.

In the years that followed, Rachel tried to find Joshua. He had moved out of his cold water flat on 10th Avenue, without even a single sock left on the floor, or a ring around the immense sink which had doubled as a chilly bathtub. No forwarding address had been left with the post office, the Dramatists Guild, or the hiring office at the Algonquin. Frantically, Rachel also checked police records, hospitals, newspaper files: no accounts of suicides or other sudden deaths or accidents even vaguely matched descriptions of her lost playwright.

She never wanted to return to Philadelphia. She did return, on rare occasions, to the Belasco Theater, once when Aleck Woollcott had his moments on the stage as an actor in S.N. Behrman's *Brief Moment*. That was 1931, the year Belasco died, and the Shuberts bought his theater. The old stage doorman swore that the ghost of Belasco, still in priestly garb, returned regularly every opening night, and the peephole mysteriously slid open at one point in the performance. Doormen who followed confirmed that this ghostly ritual continued for forty years until the Napoleonic shrine behind the peephole was ripped out to make room for heating ducts and air conditioning equipment. Or perhaps the ghost of the "Bishop of Broadway" objected to one particular opening night and decided to stop making appearances to his theatrical descendents. It was in the show-it-all year of 1971, when *Oh! Calcutta1* moved to Belasco's cherished stage, with every performer in the buff.

Rachel went to the Belasco several times in the '30s and '40s, when the curtains fell earlier on her own plays and she could watch, from the standing room area, final moments of Group Theatre productions. For ten years this astonishing company brought much passion and meaning to that platform, and made half asleep and muted citizens of the village of Broadway awake and sing. Nor did Rachel ever forgot Martita Hunt as the Countess Aurelia in Giraudoux's *The Madwoman of Chaillot,* who pointed the tip of her umbrella hopefully toward every tomorrow morning.

Rachel would fleetingly touch the short red velvet curtains hanging on brass rings behind the last row of the orchestra, and shiver slightly, remembering herself on that stage, simultaneously trying to forget. And she invariably walked up 44th Street toward Fifth Avenue, lingering under the "Algonk" marquee for an instant, acknowledging the tipped hat and half bow of the uniformed doorman, but never going inside. After she'd moved out of the Algonquin to a flat in the East Fifties, she rarely returned. The celebrated Round Table had nearly disappeared. With the coming of sound, several of the authors had unsoundly, she felt, been lured West by the moola of the movies. And other members had joined the ghostly shade of Belasco; since nobody ever suggested the table be used for a seance, their spectral wit remained in the nether world.

Ludwig Kronheim, undaunted by his initial Broadway disaster, organized a repertory company, to star Rachel, to get her before the public in classical works, many which Woollcott had predicted she would play one day. She wanted to do *new* plays, she insisted, or where else is tomorrow coming from? But Kronheim steered her toward the "safer" territory of established drama, trying to induce her to forget what he considered "a totally forgettable new playwright." For three years their collaboration became celebrated, both of their names in lights, acclamation for her inspired performances, recognition of his non-goulash direction.

Rehearsals were actually nightmares of non-collaboration, but eventually Rachel soft-talked her director into shortening what she called his "On-Too-Long" lectures to each cast, joking that was the translation of "Kronheim" into Mandarin. He finally came around and paid more attention to basics, to blocking and interpretation.

Rachel and Kronheim went separate ways after rehearsals or performances. But when their fame as a team became widespread, he suggested they become a permanent offstage combination as well.

"You are magnificent as St. Joan," he said, taking her hand, which she pulled away. "Shaw himself would be shattered with a joy he never knew if he could see you. You are beautiful. Inspiring. Saintly. I watch you and I want to rush on stage, rescue you from the flames, and take you in my arms."

Rachel looked out of the side of her eyes at this overacted, somewhat dithyrambic, seemingly sincere, insincere praise.

"But," he continued, "once the curtain is down, must you continue all this saintly horseshit?"

"What are you talking about?"

"I want to marry you, or not marry you, up to you. But I don't want to go home alone anymore. I want to go home with you. Be with you. Sleep with you. Make love to you."

"You're proposing to me, and not proposing to me in the same breath, with a little proposition stuck in the middle. Is that the idea, Ludwig?"

"We're a team: I read that in the papers all the time. Pretty soon I want to arrange a great tour—all over Europe, all over the world. Wouldn't it be terrible if in London or Paris or Vienna or Rome, we said goodnight like we do here, and go to separate rooms, even separate hotels?"

Rachel shook her head. "We don't always get along on stage in that sweetness-and-light way our press agent keeps blabbering about. What makes you think we'd get along across a breakfast table, or in bed? And for performances like that, I don't think I could stand all the rehearsals, or opening nights."

"But I think I'm in love with you. Doesn't that count?"

"Sure it counts, and I thank you, Ludwig. But I'd have to love back, and I don't. I've *got* to love the person I sleep with. Even when I sleep alone. I finally realized not long ago the main cause of insomnia—it's when you toss all night with a wide-awake nightmare realizing you don't love yourself very much, let alone *like* yourself."

XVIII.

JED and Kati visited their mentor regularly, three times a week, to listen, to learn. They sat on the floor at Rachel's feet, or paced around her golden chair. She waved her arms in the air, shouting then whispering, painting word pictures to inspire Kati's vocal chords and Jed's typewriter fingers.

"My favorite size class," Rachel said. "One. Or, at the most, two. I can reach you directly with no peripheral distractions. No listless unlistening ears. No bored eyes. I've suffered through that in larger classrooms, where a mass of non-learners bury themselves in inattention."

Rachel called to her secretary, who doubled as her cook, to roll in a portable blackboard, complete with clean eraser and sticks of white chalk.

"You first, child," she directed Kati. "Go to the board, take chalk, and write one word—large as you can."

Kati got up, walked to the blackboard, poised a stick of chalk, and waited until Rachel exploded a single word which resounded in the air of the golden room.

"PASSION!"

The white chalk dug passionately into the black of the board.

"And you can add an exclamation point. That word is for you, too, Jedediah. But more of them—for both of you. Go. Write, writer!"

The board was already crowded with the height of that first shouted word. Jed took the stick of chalk and wrote along the fringes of the board the staccato dictation Rachel flung at him like ringing notes of music:

"WATCH!
LISTEN!
ABSORB!
SEARCH!
BELIEVE!
DARE!!!"

Jed and Kati sank down at her feet again, both excited and out of breath. Rachel leaned her head back on her chair and closed her eyes, a bit exhausted from shouting her watchwords.

"I always heard you were a great teacher," Kati said gratefully. "And I knew it when I first read this." She drew her copy of Rachel's book, *How to Act a Song*, from her shoulder bag. "But I never thought I would ever, ever, ever be able to sit right here and watch, and listen, and absorb, and search, and believe, and dare—PASSION-ATELY."

Rachel took the book, turned it in her fingers, not opening it. "You know why I wrote this? To teach myself, to remind myself: what I thought I'd already learned and practiced, but had forgotten a long time ago. So actually I'm not a teacher at all. I'm a REMINDER."

Kati tentatively dared to make a suggestion. "Maybe you should flip a coin and write a book like this called *How to Sing a Scene.*

Rachel laughed. "Of course I should. And maybe I will some day—in my old age, when I have nothing else to do, after I've retired, though I never intend to."

"Thank God," Jed said, "and lucky us."

Rachel turned the pages of her book. "That's lovely advice. Some publisher might want to reissue this, if we tack on a second half, so the double book could be like a set of literary Siamese twins. You see what a wonderful two-way street this whole reminder business is? I learn so much from my students. If I listen to them occasionally."

They laughed and kissed each other.

"It's not too bad an idea, actually. I've gone back and forth all my life, and I'm still backing and forthing. I was primarily a singer at first, then primarily an actress for a lot of years, then I realized I was primarily *both*. So when musical theater in America began to bloom and burst out so beautifully, I joined up, of course, as an actress-singer. And I started to write this book."

"You're helping all of us," Jed told her. "Not just actors or singers or actor-singers or singer-actors, but writers, too. My Uncle Joshua wrote me some letters which I just got a month or so ago. You're underlining all his words, bringing them to life, making me want to start to write a play. I don't know what it's going to be about, but I'll find out. Maybe you'll help me find out."

"Of course I will. Start. Do it. Now. Soon. Your Great Uncle would want you to. *I* want you to."

She took their hands, life hanging on to life.

"I wish you two were *my* grandnephew and grandniece. Or my grandchildren. I wish I had populated the world with beautiful playwriters—that's what Belasco used to call them—and sons and daughters and grandchildren and great-grandchildren of playwriters, and even a few singer-actresses and actress-singers."

Softly Kati asked, "Did you ever have children of your own?"

Suddenly Rachel seemed far away. She dropped their

hands as if disconnecting herself from the past, as if leaving her golden room.

"Yes. One. Once. No. Never. I don't know. I don't remember. I'm not sure."

XIX.

WHEN she was alone, Rachel was never lonely. She'd sit at her golden piano and play for an appreciative audience: herself. And she was a brilliant conversationalist, but hating monologues or soliloquies, she turned to dialogue, playing scenes, the past talking to the present, the present talking to the future. They were never one character plays: there were multiple parts and she got to play all of them.

She spoke wise and often witty words, in the Algonquin Round Table tradition, some so forthright and even scatological that she would never have spoken aloud in public.

"The only way we can give birth to the future is to let the past and the present sleep together—instead of just masturbating the moment."

And she laughed at her own wit. But often she wouldn't laugh at all. When she thought of the year 1934, she slammed down the polished top of the piano keyboard, trying to shut out the dissonance of that year, to erase it from the autobiography of her music.

"Lady," one chiding side of the duologue said, "forget that terrible year. Why don't you close the play? Stop trying to revive it. It should never have opened in the first place."

"But shouldn't everything, off stage and on, have some

kind of structure? I don't mean happy endings or even tearing-your-eyes-out katharsis, but a shape, an Act I, Act II, Act III progression, some kind of sensible order and meaning."

"Not necessarily. Once Cocteau was asked if every play should have a beginning, a middle, and an end. He said: 'Of course. But not necessarily in that order.'"

"But why can't I take 1934 out of town and rewrite it? Cut out the bad scenes. Not the singing-in-the-woods part: that I want to remember, that I want to keep in. But I can't restage the rest, because maybe it never really happened. I didn't want it to happen. Please, please, somebody, some playwriter maybe, tell me I never played the unplayable part."

* * *

The 1933-34 theater season began with what the trade-papers called "A whirlwind tour from coast to coast for Broadway's great star-lady, Madame Rachel, and her marquee star mate-director, Ludwig Kronheim, warming up for an invasion of the showplaces of Europe." Rachel objected at first to the tacked on "Madame" before her singular name, claiming it was an unlikely combination of a hostess of a whorehouse and some nose-in-the-clouds French noblewoman. But the bookers and publicists were persistent and the "Madame" stuck, even later on the title page of her book.

With sufficient huzzahs for her director, Rachel illuminated stages everywhere she played. The Hanna Theater stage in Cleveland blazed more brightly than anything the theatrically minded there ever witnessed, until later years when the polluted oil slick on the Cuyahoga River burst into flame. The Blackstone in Chicago had lines at the box office, despite the biting November winds off Lake Michigan. Denver claimed her as the greatest discovery of pure silver since the mother-lode days. The Biltmore, the sole legitimate theater in movie mad Los Angeles, was packed to the second balcony for its entire two week run.

Both of them received offers from Universal, from M.G.M., from Warner Brothers, from Paramount, from United Artists, from R.K.O. Republic "passed," not quite visualizing Madame Rachel on a horse. Harry Cohn at Columbia claimed his studio wasn't interested in that "artsy-schmartsy drek." The other major studio offers included plans for star and director in tandem. Louella printed daily items in her column, as if the new star-lady's movies were already in the can. Great epics were announced, including Joan of Arc, unsullied by Shaw.

Kronheim rushed to accept the best offer. Rachel declared unequivocally that she'd only play St. Joan if the screenplay were the G.B.S. playscript intact. As for any other roles, she would insist on script approval, film by film, and no long-term contract which would keep her off the living stage every season. On that basis, every studio backed out.

A furious Kronheim took a less financially remunerative deal for himself, with or without Rachel, one picture at a time, the option on the second film depending on the success of the first. Of course beginning work on that first one would have to wait until their European tour was completed in September of 1934.

Their tour began with a gala performance in Brussels on New Year's Eve, 1933. En route on the *Île de France*, Rachel and Kronheim had kept to their separate staterooms, hardly talking to each other at hasty meals, the chill of their relationship matched only by the elements outside on their wintry crossing.

But Brussels was a triumph and warmed up their theater partnership, at least momentarily, making both of them forget their split about pouring their talents into the maw of the movies. The already celebrating turn-of-the-year audience gave them a standing ovation at the end of each act, threw flowers onto the stage at the final curtain, wanted to pull their new found goddess of the theater through the streets in an open carriage, but were stopped by a snowstorm. Belgian royalty bowed to her as she bowed to them in their royal box. In a never previously performed ritual, critics streamed backstage, one of them proclaiming loudly the essence of his review, which she could read in print "next year" on January 2, 1934: "Madame Rachel is the new Duse, an even more glorious Bernhardt, the First Lady of Theater of the Universe."

1934 had already begun by the time Rachel and Kronheim reached the ballroom of the Royal Windsor Hotel for the combined Opening Night and New Year's Eve celebration. She clung to his arm, suddenly grateful to him for arranging this already triumphant tour. When the celebrants applauded and cheered their entrance, she made Ludwig take a bow, and even kissed his cheek. The champagne filled Mayor of Brussels, his raised hand quieting the tumult, made an official and slightly officious declaration in broken English.

"We are welcoming to the great city of Bruxelles," he declaimed, "the supremest of the stars, the great Madame Rachel and her equal of the theater talents, the great *régisseur,* her husband, Monsieur Ludwig Kronheim."

Rachel was unable to correct the Mayor's florid but innacurate tribute because of the cheers which followed. But what the hell: it was the start of a new year, and what difference did it make? She reached for a glass of champagne. Apologetically, they told her the champagne was all gone. Every jeroboam in the place had been drunk up by the already drunken celebrants. Horrors! No champagne at Brussels' leading hotel? That was like saying there was no holy water at the Vatican. They offered to wake up every vintner in the city, plough through the snowdrifts and open every wine cellar in the Grand Place. She waved away their adoring courtesy and accepted vodka instead, which they assured her was "the best in Europe, including any you will find in the wilds of Moscow."

Vodka-induced dizziness made her impervious to the compliments spilling over her while more and more vodka was poured into her glass.

Each compliment also included a toast to her, in French, in Flemish, occasionally in English: "*Bonne Année! Happy 1934! Happy, beautiful 1934!*"

When she was too vodka befuddled even to lift her glass in response, the waving but wobbly Rachel was led out of the ballroom by Kronheim and into the elevator. When they reached her room, she passed out on the bed.

Her uninvited "husband" stayed the night.

XX.

AFTER Brussels, there were triumphs in Amsterdam, Copenhagen, Oslo, Stockholm. In Paris in April, Jouvet, the great French actor-director, leapt to the stage of the Théâtre Antoine as the curtain fell on *St. Joan*. He declared in eloquent French that the 20th Century Rachel had surpassed her namesake, that "we have witnessed, *bon Dieu*, our blessed Saint speaking in Shaw's gutteral English, yet the American Rachel's Jeanne d'Arc is the pinnacle of universal art."

On the train headed for Zurich, through the French then Swiss Alps, each changing moment the compartment window framed a masterpiece of soaring mountain sculpture. Scenery farther east and south would have been equally pleasing to the eyes, but far less to the mind, Rachel thought as she leaned her head against the white antimacassar on the plush upholstery. After Hitler's alliance with Mussolini in Venice, Kronheim had cancelled Rome; Berlin and Vienna had not been scheduled at all.

Now Moscow and Leningrad must be forgotten, too; and what a pity, for she longed to meet and even study fleetingly with Constantin Stanislavsky. And their summer-long climactic booking at the Haymarket in London must also be erased. After Zurich the rest of the company must be booked for passage back to the States.

When Kronheim knocked at the door of her compartment, Rachel decided, at long last, to tell him why.

"I don't remember, but I'm sure you remember, Herr Kronheim, what happened after our opening night in Brussels."

"Of course I remember. It was New Year's Eve, the start of this glorious year and this glorious tour."

"This glorious year is about to end. And so is this glorious tour. I'll play one week only in Zurich, and that's it."

"Are you sick? Your face looks so thin, my beloved Rachel. The tour has been too strenuous. We'll postpone Moscow for a week and have ourselves a vacation."

"The vacation will be permanent."

"Why? England all summer will be the climax, the mountaintop of your career in the theater, and mine too. After London we'll sail for New York, and when we reach Hollywood they'll cheer us as double stars of the entire world. I'll get them to give me a subject matter you'll love. Romance. Significance. Music. Excitement. A great screen epic to match the size of you. Anything we want! With our triumphs, especially in London, they'll lick our hands, they'll kiss our feet."

"You may go and burn in the hell of Hollywood, and if they still want to kiss anything, you tell them they may kiss my ass! Kronheim, I don't even want to see you again. In Europe. In America. At the North Pole. On the moon."

"Kings and Queens are bowing to you. The royalty of the theater are taking second billing to your genius. And you are saying words to me as if you were a guttersnipe."

"Kronheim knows what happened. *I* didn't. Not until a month later, not for sure until two months later. I still don't believe it: a sneak attack in the dark of morning, that first day of the Year of our Lord, 1934."

"An inevitability. I've always wanted to make love to you. That night especially, I didn't want you to be alone."

"I'm not alone anymore."

She ripped open the front of her long silken robe.

"Look! Look at the opening night present Kronheim gave his 'beloved Rachel.' You say I'm thin. I'm no longer thin all over."

Kronheim moved toward her as if to embrace her. She pulled away from him, sank to the compartment seat, turned her back on him.

He spoke in a low tone, concise, businesslike.

"You've hidden your condition admirably. We can continue to do so. We'll get you new costumes, there are designers who can make anything disappear—with long flowing robes. We'll get married in Zurich or whenever you say. And our tour will continue. It *must* continue."

When she turned to face him again, she was crying and laughing at the same time, with a cutting edge of sarcasm in her voice.

"Oh, absolutely. I'll tell you the exact date I want to marry you, you son of a bitch: NEVER! But dear Regisseur Kronheim, let us join hands in planning the grand opening in London, with our precious little bastard child still under wraps. By all means invite George Bernard Shaw to sit in the Royal box. He's 84, he's lived long enough, this will kill him instantly. What a dramatic triumph: the Maid of Orléans at the stake, a mere seven months pregnant, about to ascend to heaven, clutching her bulging belly, the second most famous immaculate conception in religious history."

Kronheim pressed his lips together so rigidly it seemed they would never open again. When they did, he spoke with acid sweetness.

"What a scene! Quite a scene! Who wrote that? Some

Hungarian? No. Strindberg maybe. Or Gerhart Haupt-
mann. Not funny enough to be Ibsen; he'd have put in
more jokes. I'd really prefer Schnitzler, or at least Molnar.
Pirandello! That's it! He writes stuff where nobody ever
knows what really happened."

Rachel got up, tightening her robe around herself. She
pushed past him. With superstrength generated by fury,
she slid open the compartment door and shoved
Kronheim into the train corridor. Then she yanked the
sliding door shut, getting him out of her sight, trying to
erase him from her life.

XXI.

BOTH attempted calm in Zurich as they ended their "triumphant tour." Rachel played her final week as St. Joan, without passion, often with her back to the audience, never in profile. The response was polite but not ecstatic. "What caused the reported excitement in Paris and elsewhere?" one critic wrote in *Schweizer Deutsch*, the language of Eastern Switzerland. "Why bring this tepid performance to our 'Athens on the Limmat?' Jeanne d'Arc without fire seems dead long before the flames consume her."

Kronheim tried to be conciliatory, even kind, but his smile was always forced as he bowed acceptance. He sent the rest of the American company home. He arranged for Rachel to have her promised "vacation" by renting her a tiny chalet close to the wooded border between Switzerland and Austria. He would take an office in Zurich to wind up their affairs. After that, what? Perhaps all their problems would melt like the spring Alpine snows.

The best part of this arrangement, Kronheim enthused, was that his warm and wonderful sister Erna lived in an Austrian village just across the border. She was a midwife and could come visit Rachel, bringing advice on borning babies along with her homemade küchen and apple strudel. Her credentials were impressive. She had brought nearly a hundred children into the world and at least a thousand pieces of strudel.

Rachel found momentary peace in her chalet and in the countryside around it. She could walk through the woods to the nearest village, Oberplatz, where the post office seemed no larger than a postage-stamp. But who needed post offices? She had decided not to give anybody her address and not to write any letters to "the outside world." She enjoyed the goat cheese in tiny barrels she could tote back through the woods, and the superchocolate chocolates which she felt he?/she? must be enjoying too. At first she didn't like the cuckoo clock above the chalet fireplace; it was a toy gargoyle, which impertinently poked its head out and squawked on the hour. But she began to enjoy it, and she talked to it. "You know you're cuckoo," she'd tell it. "But who isn't?"

Rachel came to appreciate Kronheim's sister Erna, who made regular calls across the border. She was a sweet lady, with a bun of absolutely golden hair, the prototype of every woman in history who ever wore a bun. Erna was soft-spoken, a cook who made Rachel's stomach never want to take any nourishment again that wasn't Erna's strudel or küchen. Though she had never had any children of her own, Erna spoke warmly about borning beautiful babies. But why did they always cry? Didn't they realize they were loved and wanted and welcome?

Kronheim came from Zurich to Oberplatz only once, trying to be amusing, laughing about the name of the village, ("Is there also an *Unter*platz somewhere in the neighborhood?") but Rachel never laughed at his attempted wit, only at his continued and persistent proposals of marriage, and his insistence that she sail back to America with him. Now. Soon.

"It will solve everything," he said with studied conviction. "We will arrive home, man and wife. Naturually, the baby will be born in California. A month later you will begin shooting your first picture."

"If, Kronheim, you are not first shot between the eyes—by me. Now, go away and let me have my vacation. I do not wish my son—*my* son, not yours!—to be born in California, or my daughter—*my* daughter, not yours. I intend to have *my* child here, in the free, uncluttered air of Switzerland, not as part of a movie deal."

"And what will you tell the screaming press when they meet your ship in New York harbor, the celebrated single mother Great Lady of the Theater, with a bundle full of bastard in her arms?"

"I'll tell them nothing, unless a fully grown bastard like you tells them first. Then I won't glorify your masculinity by announcing that you are the father. For you're not the father. Love is the father. What I was dreaming of in my vodka drunkeness, all my remembered love—that is the father. I'll simply say I'm returning from a well deserved rest, with an adopted orphan who will be much more than a child for me: a human being I can love and cherish for the rest of my life."

Kronheim left. And he never came back.

XXII.

RACHEL tried to obliterate the summer of 1934. The memories which persisted were all vague in her mind like mottled, leafy patches of sunlight through trees, as if she had stepped into a picture frame and become part of a painting by Monet.

Plenty of fresh milk was brought to her by the villagers of Oberplatz. Two old ladies cooked and cleaned; an old man worked in the garden around the chalet. Rachel's only clear and happy memory was of her daily walks in the woods, mostly in the sunshine, but even in the rain, when she lifted her head and tasted the raindrops. She sang to her unborn child, making up lullabies in her head. They were always happy melodies, sweet as the rain. Rachel believed the life inside her could hear every note she sang: it would certainly be born smiling.

Erna visited Rachel regularly. She had received one message from her brother Ludwig. He was back in America, already on a train heading for the West Coast. Rachel resisted hearing any other news, suspecting the world was coming to pieces in the Nazi-mad center of Europe, but feeling she and her baby would be safe in neutral Switzerland. But one day, as Erna left, a hint of terror filled her usually peaceful eyes.

"What's wrong, Erna? Tell me."

"I do not wish you to worry," Erna said, not looking

directly at Rachel. "I will be back, every week, and for a whole week in September when your baby is born. I will be here. I promise. I will get through, even if the border is closed."

"What's happened? This time I want to know."

Erna spoke with difficulty. "In Deutschland a plebiscite has declared Herr Hitler their Führer. And yesterday, in my country, the Austrian Nazis assassinated our Chancellor Dollfuss."

* * *

The border wasn't closed yet in early August. Erna was back for the unexpected day and night of long and painful labor when Rachel's baby was born prematurely.

Rachel remembered nothing but the pain. What had Erna given her? Pills to put her to sleep? A shot to try to take away the pain? Why? It was happy pain and she wanted to stay awake to welcome her baby to the world.

When she woke, there was light in the sky. Erna was gone and there was no baby in Rachel's arms. She looked around the room in panic. The two old women of the village were there. One came to the bed with a damp cloth to wipe the perspiration from her forehead. She clutched the woman's arm.

"Where's my baby?"

"*Tot,*" the old woman whispered. "*Gestorben.*"

"In English. Tell me in English!"

Awkwardly, the other old woman moved closer, taking Rachel's hand, struggling to get the words out in halting English. "So small. So thin. It is in *himmel*, in heaven. *Das Kindchen*, your baby, it died."

The words went around in Rachel's head like a maniac merry-go-round spinning off its track.

"He/she/it died. It died. She died. He died. She was too small to live. He was too thin to live. Eight-ninths of a baby. Gone. Never really born. So it never lived. But how can you die if you've never been born? Stay unborn, everybody, then you'll never have to die! Hide in Mama's tummy. Stay there. Safe. Who wants to be born these days? Wouldn't it be wonderful if Hitler had never been born? *Il Duce*, climb back into your mama mia's womb! Stay there alongside the fettucini-like Fallopian tubes, Musso, so someday they won't have to hang you like a salami by the heels. No Russian lullabies for you, Comrade Stalin. If you'd only had the sense to let your mamuchka drop you as a gross miscarriage of justice!"

She died. He died. It died. If it had been twins, *they* would have died too.

XXIII.

RACHEL never told anybody about her lost summer in Switzerland or about her lost child. With selective memory and deliberate forgetfulness, she didn't tell Jed and Kati either, except that when she had recovered from her "exhausting rest cure," she returned to New York to make plans for the rest of the century. And she bought this house, filling it with the glint of gold for everything from bathroom fixtures to walls and ceilings and her grand piano, her golden piano.

She announced to the press and the newsreel cameramen that she was settling permanently in New York, hoping to do a new play this year, a new musical next year, a classical play the following year, then a musical, a play, a musical, a play, for the rest of her natural life. Happily the world of theater art caught up with her, just around the turn of the '40s, when American composers and lyricists and bookwriters invented and developed and produced *both* at once: musical plays, MUSICAL THEATER!

"Of course, and you know damn well, a lot had happened earlier," Rachel told Jed and Kati with enthusiastic near-scholarly enjoyment. "There were grace notes to the greatness of the form, breakthroughs like *Show Boat*, and *Music in the Air* before that, and almost operas like *Porgy and Bess*. And suddenly we had ourselves a born-and-bred in America art form. The only other ones I can think of are jazz and tall-tales or even the appropriate deliciously dirty joke. Pure American, all of them. Or even not so pure."

"The reason I ran away from the convent is I wanted to sing the music you're talking about," Kati beamed, "not just holy hymns. I found out about it when Sister Gert, Sister Maria I mean, turned me into an O.C.A. freak."

"Oh, I know all about you Original Cast Album freaks," Rachel laughed. "I'm one, too! President of the sorority, I think. Chief honorary freak of the fraternity."

She waved her hand toward a long cabinet, which filled the wall on the opposite side of the room.

"Open those, Jedediah. You'll see what I mean."

Jed turned the gold handles and flung open the cabinet doors. They saw rows of thick 78-RPM cast albums, then long lines of LP's, graduating to shiny new CD's, with accompanying record players and turntables, mixers and amplifiers.

"There they are," Rachel declaimed, "every O.C.A. ever recorded and reissued, in all sizes and shapes and speeds, all designed to make music come out of the mouths of multiple speakers into our created-in-heaven stereophonic ears."

"Oh, God, God, they're wonderful," Kati breathed, touching the edges of the albums as if they were religious relics. "I just want to lie on the floor and listen to every one of them right now."

"That 'right now' might take you ten years, child, but help yourself, any ten years you choose."

They laughed and kissed each other again.

"They're modern day miracles, do you know that? Nobody thought of recording original cast albums until 1942, when Jack Kapp at Decca decided he'd take a flyer at *Oklahoma*, and Rodgers & Hammerstein said okay, let's try it, and everybody said nobody'd buy it, but they did, and it all lived happily ever after, not just in that first four record 78, but there in the LP's and down the line in CD. And we're still doing it, even when there's not much left to do. Thank you, Jack!"

With a flourish, as if trumpets should be sounding, she flung a salute to heaven or thereabouts.

"I remember the first time I went into the Decca recording studios. There, high on the wall, Jack had hung a large painting of the Vanishing American: a half-naked Indian, astride a horse, arms flung to heaven, framed by a dying sunset, moving slowly to his grave and, it seemed, toward the death of everything beautiful. His mouth seemed to be shaping words, as if crying out for something forever lost. Jack had splashed, in large type, across the bottom of the painting:

WHERE'S THE MELODY?

"Of course, Jack bannered that motto to make sure arrangers and orchestrators wouldn't bury all the beautiful tunes of the time under a lot of hoopla and noisy ear-shattering musical irrelevancies. But we sure as hell need that motto now. These days the melodies themselves have vanished."

Jed and Kati tried to convince Rachel to put all of this into a new book: an update of *How to Act a Song*, coupled with Kati's idea for the second half: *How to Sing a Scene*.

"I'm not really very good as a writer," Rachel protested.

"Good writing is just good talking," Jed said. Talk to your reader, one on one, the way you're talking to us."

"Oh, I can talk all right. Sometimes, even when I'm by myself, I talk so much, I look around for a button or a switch to turn myself off."

"Everything you say turns *us* on," Kati said, waving Rachel's book, "and we all need a double whammy edition of this."

"If you claim you can't write, which I don't believe," Jed persisted, "how'd you write that one?"

"I didn't write it, I dictated it."

"Same thing. You don't need a pencil or a typewriter or a sharp stick in wet cement or even a goddam word processor to get what you're thinking or saying into print. It just has to be good. Only one requirement: it shouldn't bore the shit out of you. No chance of that here."

Jed took some folded sheets of yellow legal pad paper out of his pocket and poised his pen.

"Talk! I'm an eloquent listener."

"You want to be my 'as told to' scribbler? I'll insist that you take credit."

"Nope. I want to put down *your* words, not mine, try to catch the melody of what you're saying on paper."

She stared at him for a moment.

"My God, you really are your uncle's great-nephew. More like his son, or his grandson. You even talk like him a little." Her eyes lit up. "What would you think if we dedicated the book to him?"

"If you did that, I'd get it all down ten times as fast, a hundred times as passionately."

"I'm glad you like the idea."

"Like it! Why the hell do you think we came 3,000 miles? Meeting you, being with you, is my heirloom from my uncle. Start talking."

XXIV.

TWO months of talking and scribbling filled a golden book of stories and legends of life in the theater plus a smattering of reach-back-and-try-to-recapture-it theatrical wisdom, born-with or acquired. Rachel never dispensed the usual "do-exactly-as-I-did" advice, more "what-not-to-do-and-how-not-to-do-it-beautifully."

And there were vivid visions of special moments on the stage of the Belasco Theater 62 years before.

Were all the legends true? Who cared? They were tributes to theater performers, a storehouse of stories in Rachel's head, not ever jokes, but character comedies about real life characters she'd loved, on stage and off.

"Ethel Waters was one of the most beautiful-comic, comic-beautiful great ladies I ever saw on a stage. She could get spitting mad, but most of the time she had a kind of passionate quiet, deep inside her. And I think she kept prompting God to be sure to stay awake and keep his eye on the fall of every sparrow.

"At the tag end of the '40s, heading into the '50s, the great director Harold Clurman (though not everybody always agreed with him) directed Ethel Waters in Carson McCuller's incredibly beautiful play, *Member of the Wedding*. It only played 50 performances, but I must have seen at least ten of them. I loved the play, and I loved the theater, too: the Empire, which was my favorite playhouse, after the Belasco, of course. But the sons of bitches tore it down, long before it was fashionable to tear down theaters. And look at what they've put up instead: hotels! office buildings! I couldn't possibly perform in an office building; I'd feel like a filing cabinet!

"But I was talking about Ethel Waters, wasn't I? Well, all during rehearsals of *Member of the Wedding* she just *marked* her part, and Clurman began to get worried. Just before they headed to Philadelphia—to the Forrest, by God, pre-Christmas, 1949—he asked her to stay after their final New York rehearsal."

The moments she described came alive to Jed, as if he were seeing it all through a peephole, Belasco fashion.

"Miss Waters," Clurman said. "I've got to talk to you."

"Sit down, Mr. Clurman honey." He pulled up a chair alongside hers. The worklight on the empty rehearsal stage lit the face of a beaming black madonna.

"The stage picture I see of you, Miss Waters, is absolutely beautiful. When you cradle Julie or Brandon in your lap, you look like the *Pieta*. But frankly you are mumbling and all your words are lost. The other actors claim they can hardly hear their cues. We open in Philadelphia in four days. Carson has written a wonderful play and you simply must come up to the level of a performance."

"Mr. Clurman, I want to tell you a little story about the animals in the jungle, all of them partying one hot summer afternoon. All except Mr. Lion, slumbering in the shade. And the other animals said: 'How come Mr. Lion not dancing and cavorting with us?' So they sent Mr. Elephant over to inquire politely: 'Mr. Lion. You're the King of the Beasts. How come you're sitting out all the partying in the warm afternoon sunshine?' And hardly opening his eyes, Mr. Lion said: 'Mr. Elephant, in the cool of the evening, when the humping begins, I'll be there!'"

She was there all right; she came on like gangbusters. The Philadelphia critics cheered the author-playwright, the director, the unforgettable cast: Julie Harris, seven-year-old Brandon de Wilde, but especially Ethel Waters. Frederick de Wilde, young Brandon's father, who was production stage manager, reported what happened a week later, on Christmas Eve just before the performance. He was listening, in a corridor in the Forrest annex, when she called Julie and Brandon into her dressing room, and he overheard, word-for-word, her fervent Christmas prayer.

"Children, get down on your knees."

Puzzled, Julie and the boy did. Eyes to heaven, Ethel Waters also sank to her knees, clasping her hands.

"Dear Lord, here we are in the City of Brotherly Love. Merry Christmas, dear God. May your light shine on Miss Julie Harris, who's like an angel in your city of gold. And Lord love Mr. Brandon de Wilde, who's like one of your heavenly cherubs. And Lord bless Miss Carson McCullers who wrote this beautiful, beautiful play. And, oh, dear sweet Lord, don't let Mr. Harold Clurman fuck it up!"

* * *

"Ethel Waters was an inspired performer," Rachel said, "on stage and even in her dressing room. She was a singer who acted a song, an actress who sang a scene. I guess she drove directors crazy, because she waited for audiences; then she lullabied all of them, not lulling them to sleep, but gently rocking them awake.

"If we're still writing this book—are we?—she's the perfect example of the 'double whammy' part. Because every scene, like every song, has got to *go* someplace, not just sit there like a dead cabbage leaf."

Kati was all wound up. "Before I read your book, the

already printed part, all I'd ever studied was some Stanislavsky, *An Actor Prepares* mostly. And I'd rehearse like crazy, trying to figure out the subtext of every word of every lyric and why a note was sharped instead of flatted, but sometimes it all got so complicated I forgot what I was singing. Then I met *you* on paper and after that I just went out and *did* it."

"That's it. That's it, Kati. Of course you have to prepare, to rehearse. You have to know who you are and where you are and when you are. And where you're going! It's a trip, child, with both meanings of that word. Sure, Mr. Stanislavsky tells you to pack up what luggage you need, but he doesn't ever tell you to *schlep* it all on stage with you, until you're weighed down like Atlas with the whole heavy world on your shoulders."

Jed's pencil kept racing, getting down as much as he could: Rachel's words, her stories, her ideas. What an inheritance!

"I keep thinking about Paul Muni, who used to say the same thing. Great actor. Hell of a musician, too. Munya, that's what we used to call him, began acting at the age of 12, old men usually, and playing the fiddle, too. And he used all the strings of his talent brilliantly. When he became a famous star, people asked him: 'How do you do it, Mr. Muni? What's your method?' And he'd smile and say: 'My grandmother made the best apple strudel of anybody, anywhere. When they asked for her recipe, she'd say: 'Easy. I get up in the morning, I wash my hands, I put on my apron, and I bake apple strudel." And that's how I act.'"

Rachel closed her eyes for a moment. "When I hear that word, I always think of the best apple strudel *I* ever ate—it couldn't have been Munya's grandmother's—in Switzerland, in Oberplatz."

Jed looked up from his lined yellow paper as Rachel hastily corrected herself.

"In a *village*, where I went to recuperate from what they called in those days 'a nervous breakdown.' They cured me with the Swiss-Austrian equivalent of latter-day penicillin: good old apple strudel. Tons of it. ' Absolutely unnerving."

Jed felt intuitively, as Rachel stared at him, that she didn't want him to write down any of this. But he knew she had inadvertenly said the strange, funny name of that Swiss village, "Oberplatz," then covered it up quickly. He folded his notepaper and put it into his pocket. He swore to himself he'd never ask her about it, never invade what must be an area of vulnerability. But Jed sensed that some day he'd find out.

XXV.

"BE an original!" Rachel almost shouted to her Boswell, cross-legged on the floor, and to the kneeling would-be actress-singer, singer-actress, drinking in her future.

"Don't be a carbon copy of anybody or anything! Oh, that dates me, doesn't it? I should say 'Xerox,' shouldn't I? But, remember, I still say 'icebox'. And I still call all those gizmos over there a 'Victrola'."

She always smiled her advice. "Of course sometimes being an original gets you into a publicly acclaimed groove, so you keep imitating that original originality for the rest of your life. And it doesn't always pay off. You go backwards so often you end up kicking yourself in the *tochus*. That's Yiddish, dear: an indispensible and highly descriptive language you can't get along without, not in this business. *Tochus* simply means that lovely curved surface of your body, just behind you and slightly below the waist; it's where your lap goes when you stand up."

Jed illustrated by lovingly running his fingers down Kati's back as if it were a piano keyboard. Playfully, she slapped his hand.

"The inspired Chaplin is the perfect example of what I'm talking about," Rachel glowed. "Part clown, part mime, part ballet dancer, all actor, all MUSIC of the muscles and the mind.

"Do you know the absolutely true story about Charlie? When his Little Tramp became world famous, a vaudeville theater in downtown Los Angeles decided to hold a Chaplin look-alike contest. Hundreds entered. Charlie was so fascinated with the notion, that he decided to put on his floppy pants, his tilted derby, his elegant tramp costume. Twirling his curving cane and twitching his mustache, he entered the contest himself. He came in third!"

* * *

It was what Rachel called "late in the run" of their increasingly numerous sessions that Jed asked her to tell them more about his Uncle's long forgotten play, *The Mandarin Lady*.

"Nothing more to tell."

"I've been trying to find a copy of the script," Jed said. "Everywhere. No library has a trace of it. There's a tiny mention of it in the 1930–31 *Burns Mantle Best Plays*, but not a shred of the play itself."

"There are no copies. Anywhere. Joshua tore up or burned them all. Even mine."

Rachel's voice seemed far away, two generations ago.

"But I remember a lot of it, especially the end of Act III. Plays were always in three acts in those days. In the first act, I was a young Chinese mother. In the second act, the baby I'd held in my arms was all grown up: my son was now a writer who kept searching, to the past to try to inherit some wisdom, to the future where the way, the Tao, might take him, always trying to find some essence of truth. Oh, there was a long intermission between Act II and Act III, when a make-up expert piled on gobs of greasepaint, and creased my face with liners to make wrinkles deeper than time. I became a kind of universal earth mother, the most ancient creature anybody had ever seen."

Transformed by Rachel's vivid description, Jed and Kati seemed to be sitting in plush red seats of the Belasco Theater on closing night of *The Mandarin Lady* in the fall of 1930. They watched a mature Chinese writer at the foot of a series of levels, which pyramided into the overhead dark, as he peered into the unknown. The writer came downstage, pleading to God or the gods.

"Please. Once, just once, let me look into the face of Truth."

An echoing, disembodied voice rumbled like distant thunder from the skies. "Come with me. I will show you Truth."

A spot hit the first level. The writer, lured to it, climbed upward. When he turned forward, looking into the light, a kaleidoscope of colors played on his face, whirling, blending, changing, sunsets turning into rainbows, sunrises exploding into multicolored Chinese fireworks. The writer marveled. "Such colors, such beautiful colors. Colors I've never seen before. Colors beyond the spectrum of the rainbow." And he clapped his hands, the joyful discoverer. "Ah! This is the truth of being a writer: to see something *nobody else* has ever seen before and to be able to describe it all in words."

The disembodied voice called to him. "This is only a way stop. Come. I shall show you more. Climb higher, toward the clouds, toward the stars."

The whirling colors faded as a spot hit a second level, where the climbing writer's feet seemed to be touching moving clouds. He breathed in deeply, his lungs filling with beautifully scented air.

"Such perfumes! Such magical perfumes! Aromas I've never known before, so overpowering I not merely inhale them, smell them, experience them with *one* sense, but I *see* them! Like pillars of ice and fire." His head swirled as if keeping time to a wonderful melody. "And I can *hear* the perfumes, like flowing music. Oh, listen to the perfume of the clouds!"

The writer stretched out his hands, stroking the velvet air. "I can *touch* them! And the perfumes are seeping into my pores, into my soul." He leaped up, a sudden surge of strength and self-knowledge. "Now I *really* know the truth of being a writer: we must experience everything we encounter not just with *one* sense, but *every* sense. Then we are true observers of the multiplicity of all we witness in our lives. And the unknown becomes known."

The unseen voice called out to him again. "Technique. Methodology. Reportage of the senses: every skillful writer knows he must use that. Come with me one step further. I will show you the face of Truth itself."

The voice mesmerized the writer to the very apex of the pyramid. There at the peak, in a great carved chair, sat the oldest woman he had ever seen. He half turned away for he saw that she was also the ugliest woman he had ever seen.

An ancient voice emerged from deep in her throat. "Come closer, my boy."

He moved toward her, almost unable to look at her.

"Are you Truth?"

"Yes, my boy. I am Truth."

"Thank you for the favor of being able to look into your face at last. Now I shall go tell the world about you."

"If you consider it a favor," she murmured, "do a favor for me in return. When you tell the world about me, tell them that I am YOUNG and BEAUTIFUL."

XXVI.

"WHY was the play a failure? Only four performances. That's criminal."

"Oh, Jedediah," Rachel said, touching his puzzled face, "a five year run doesn't turn drek into gold. Sometimes a single performance of something delicate and poetic can be an all time hit in your remembering mind."

"Then whose fault was it that it closed so quickly?"

"The audiences that weren't there, the ones who stayed away. And the few who came, including the critics. I guess they were too depressed by the Depression to listen to poetry. Your Uncle Joshua wrote the play to be designed and staged inside their heads. But the audiences resigned, fired themselves from the beautiful task of firing up their own imaginations."

"Which director really directed it? Belasco or Kronheim?"

"Both. And neither. It was really directed best on paper by the playwright. Not a lot of blocking and that 'cross downstage center' stuff. The emotional life of the characters told us where to go and what to *be*."

"What happened to Kronheim? Do you have any idea where he is now?"

"In hell, if there's any justice. In heaven, if he used a fake passport. Or in limbo or purgatory or wherever they send a combination genius-asshole. Oh, forgive the descriptive language, Kati. I say what I feel; no time left for polite euphemisms."

She shook her head, not really wanting to answer Jed's question. Taking a deep breath, she kept going. "Who knows what happened to Kronheim? I tried desperately *not* to find out. A lot of years later, in the '70s, I went on a 'pleasure trip' to Europe; I thought by then it might be possible for a trip like that to be pleasurable. But I made a helluva mistake: I got curious, I walked backward. Everything was gone: a Swiss chalet I'd stayed in for awhile, the wooded area near it cut down for lumber, the Austrian village across the border obliterated, not a building standing, even a city hall or anything resembling record books or anybody alive anywhere who had the vaguest idea about people who had lived there or died there.

"Kronheim? I managed to get scraps of information about him, but not until a long time after that. He left Europe permanently 'in time,' as they used to say. Every self-respecting artist and scientist did, whether they were Jewish, half Jewish, a quarter Jewish, or not Jewish at all. They got out of Germany and Austria and Poland and Lithuania and Czechoslovakia and Italy and, if they were lucky, to England or South Africa, or here, a lot of the writers all the way to Santa Monica Canyon by the still pacific Pacific Ocean.

"Kronheim became part of that colony of expatriates for awhile. A couple of actors told me later that they'd worked for him, for a very short time. They had bit parts in a B picture about everybody still dancing waltzes beneath crystal chandeliers in Vienna come hell, Hitler, or high water. Later Christopher Isherwood based his ironic little book, *Prater Violet*, on what happened to both Kronheim and Berthold Viertel in the movie business. Viertel was luckier, he got to direct his film on a similar theme in England, and he finished it and it was eventually released. Kronheim, in Hollywood, was yanked off his film halfway through it, and the final 'product' was junked the day Der Führer marched into the Sudetenland. That's a real half-ass way of 'making it' in Hollywood, don't you think?

"Kronheim disappeared after that. Completely. Nothing in the newspapers, nothing in *Variety*. There were vague rumors that he'd gone back to Austria to try to get some members of his family out. But that's the last I ever heard about him. I doubt if he ever got anybody out, including himself."

* * *

Jed brooded a lot about the old lady on Joshua's mountaintop. And he challenged Rachel to help him figure out what his uncle was trying to say. The reverse of the actual words? Does even the mouth of the face of truth speak lies? And wasn't it better, Jed argued, not to sugar-coat everything? Not to cover everything with diamonds or marshmallow sauce? But to try to dig beneath the gilt (or guilt?) surface of things and uncover, reveal the deceptions: the lies told us by our parents, our lovers, our government, our churches, our teachers, mostly the lies we tell ourselves. Isn't that the subject matter of an infinite number of plays?

"Of course it is," Rachel said. "But we all lie. We lie brilliantly: to make the fiction truer than the mere factual. Who tells the truth better—Shakespeare or Holinshed? Why, Will, of course. In his years as a brilliant critic, Harold Clurman defined theater perfectly in the title of one of his books: *Lies Like Truth*. Verisimiltude: that's the word. The appearance of truth. Every play should be happening *now*. This minute. In front of the audience's eyes. Not by *shlepping* in a whole Childs Restaurant, but with the passion of belief: by the playwright, by the director, by all the actors, mostly in the heads of the audience. Better than any dull, dry, dreary history book.

"Look at me. I invented myself. I made a broad from Scranton, one generation removed from a vowel-poor half-Polish, half-Russian village, into what some people call 'The Divine Rachel,' isn't that a lovely lie? And what's every good, honest, legitimate playwright? I'll tell you what he is: a DIVINE LIAR!"

Jed's pen raced to get everything down in his self-invented shorthand, shaking with excitement. Kati seemed to be soaking in every word, like Joshua's writer on his climb, listening with her elbows, her eyebrows, her kneecaps.

"Oh, children," Rachel said apologetically, "am I rattling on too much? I like to think of myself as some kind of teacher, not just passing on some nonfactual, occasionally unwise wisdom, but brushing up on my own half-remembered homework. But I don't ever want to be a pompous preacher. If you catch me sermonizing at you, or at myself, for the love of God, shut me up!"

"I've never caught you passing the collection plate," Jed assured her, "not once."

"Me neither," Kati chimed in.

"Don't put any of that 'wasn't-I-wonderful' autobiographical stuff in there," Rachel warned, pointing to Jed's pile of notes. "We're supposed to be talking about 'How to Sing a Scene'—your title for Act Two of the book, Kati. And we've said or sung damn little about that."

Jed raised the butt of his pen in the air, like a junior high school pupil asking to be called on.

"I know," he said, "that you're not suggesting Pavarotti

should play Willy Loman. But define your terms for us. Should there be a few arias in Mamet? A little recitativo by Al Pacino?"

"No. Definitely no. Come on over to the piano with me."

They sat on the piano bench, shoulder to shoulder, elbow to elbow. Rachel began improvising at the keyboard.

"Now, I don't have to be playing; you already know how much music there is in this instrument, played or waiting to be played. And a song doesn't have to be labeled a song in order to be music. When you hear a melody that's insistent and haunting, you can never get it out of your head. You even wake up in the middle of the night humming it.

"Well, it's got to be that way with every important scene and line of a play, even if the whole thing's not labeled a musical or an opera. As an actor, as a writer or director too, you have to believe in the melody of each moment, or the audience won't. They won't hear your voice, they won't hear you singing. Reaching that audience, 'that collective genius' somebody called it, is the litmus paper test. Because they know. They know if you're faking the melody, or that you're not really able to sing it. It has to reach their inner, inner guts and the insides of their brain linings, so they'll never be able to forget it, or you, or the play—then they'll want to go on living in the living theater."

XXVII.

Jed rented a one-room, sixth-floor walk-up, midtown west of 9th Avenue. In his great-uncle's day a place like this was called a cold-water flat. In this "modern age," a portable shower augmented the kitchen sink-bathtub, and a small gas watertank and a movable electric heater had been added. Jed calculated that the rent was twenty times what his uncle had probably paid. But look at what a pay phone call, a subway ride, or a trip on the Staten Island Ferry each cost then: a nickel.

He also rented the most inexpensive word processing computer he could find and went to work editing the first half and getting down the second half of Rachel's double book. He budgeted himself to five pages a day and in a perseverant month he rattled a rough first draft through his portable printer.

During that month, Kati and Rachel enjoyed daily side-by-side singing sessions, seated on the bench of the golden piano, paying tribute to the singable scores of Broadway's '40s and '50s and '60s.

"It plays on the page," a delighted Rachel told Jed after she'd read the manuscript. "Though I don't often listen to myself, it does sound the way I talk, don't you think?"

Jed nodded a happy "absolutely."

"But better!" Rachel added. "Much better. Not everybody can catch the cadence of somebody else's speech. And not everybody can write dialogue. You've done all that beautifully, adding things I intended to say but never got around to, things I might have said, should have said, wish I had said, and there it finally is, on paper. Jedediah, next you've got to write a play. Not for me. For everybody."

Now what to do with the book manuscript, where should they take it? Rachel never had an acting agent, she told them, and only once a literary agent, Jennings Morgan, who had arranged for the publication of the first half of this book. But agent, publisher, and the book itself had long since passed into the great public domain in the sky.

So Jed spent time in bookstores, used and new, finding on book spines and jackets the names of publishers who specialized in theater related subject matter. He jotted down a list of the authors of show business how-to books as well as biographies and as-told-to autobiographies of film and stage celebrities. Then he checked with the Authors Guild to find the names of their agents. He was delighted to discover that many of these books were represented by the Rich Morgan Agency. He phoned. The name Rachel opened the door for an appointment the next afternoon.

The charming businesslike Rich Morgan leafed through the manuscript, carefully noncommittal, noting that his father, Jennings Morgan, had indeed handled Rachel's original book. But after the senior Morgan's death in 1965, the agency had passed into a holding action by subordinates while the son was busy finishing prep school and getting through Dartmouth.

"We'll have a look at it," Morgan said. "Give us two or three weeks. We'll be in touch."

Exactly two weeks later, Jed was summoned for a conference. He wanted to rush right back uptown to tell Rachel about Morgan's enthusiasm for the project. "We've already made copies and sent them off to a couple of publishers. It's a fine job of writing."

"It's a fine job of talking."

Morgan waved to a shelf full of as-told-to volumes. "Lot of difference. Sometimes we've gone through three or four writers until we found the right one: somebody who knows how to *write*, not just listen. We call the other ones 'verbatim hacks.' Doesn't work."

Jed's pulse started to race. Oh, God, why hadn't he come to New York five or ten years ago?

"Tell me something," Rich Morgan asked. "How old is Madame Rachel? She's still alive, I hope."

"She's 92. A century year baby. But younger than I am. And more alive."

The agent nodded toward a stack of black and white and color photographs on his desk. Atop it was a mock-up of a book jacket for a contemplated cocktail table type volume. The title was in multicolor letters in a sweeping rainbow arc:

THE GOLDEN AGE OF MOVIE MUSICALS

"What are you doing next? Got something else in the hopper? You interested in a short-term assignment?"

"Hell, yes," Jed answered quickly.

"The front matter of this is fine. But the film historian who'd been collecting these great stills for 60 years died before he could write anything about each individual shot other than titles and star's names and dates. How'd you like to take a crack at a couple of these: a perceptive paragraph or two on each great moment of each great musical caught brilliantly by the greatest still photographers of this century? Your work would have to be on spec at first to see what you come up with. You have an agent?"

"You want the job?"

"Sure," Morgan said, pulling three loose photos out of the stack. "Let's start with these. If they're any good, you can do as many as you like, 125 in all, and we'll figure out some kind of flat fee, maybe even part of the action. Just keep the copy fresh, original, a new angle on each one. We've got a motto around this office: DEATH TO CLICHÉS. From what I've read of what you've done with Rachel's little double book, I think you subscribe to that."

Jed reached for the photos. "You got yourself a man."

"You know who these people are, of course."

"Judy? Gene Kelly? Julia Kole? Who the hell doesn't? I used to date a gal in Berkeley who never liked to go out. All she wanted to do was stay home, order fast food, and rent videotapes. I didn't mind that too much: her VCR was in her bedroom."

He shuffled the stills admiringly, holding each up to the light.

"Great musical movies. We saw them all."

They stood, shook hands.

"When do you want to see some sample copy?"

"Yesterday."

"I'll try to swing that, but I'm not sure I can make it. How about tomorrow?"

XXVIII.

JED propped the photographs alongside his computer. His caption copy for Judy Garland in *A Star is Born* flowed easily: the sophisticated lady of song breaking everybody's heart with "The Man That Got Away," years or perhaps it was only minutes later than the child-Dorothy sang "Over the Rainbow."

Gene Kelly in *An American in Paris* was even easier to write: liquid and melodic Gershwin set in motion by a master of the ever-moving musical film. Jed once read that Kelly began every conference of a borning film project with a challenge to his production colleagues: "Spill out every notion you have, that's what I'm going to do; and don't be afraid of being foolish." This free-flowing creative collaboration produced a lot of *non*-foolish ideas which made Kelly's films landmark musicals. This became the essence of Jed's Gene Kelly huzzah.

Jed turned to his third assigned star. Julia Kole in *Love Dance* danced right out of the glossy color still. It was a solo, without a partner, but she seemed to be held in a man's arms. The look in her eyes made you believe she was dancing with her imagined perfect partner, the idealized love of her life. And that's what Jed wrote about Julia Kole.

Rich Morgan approved, gave him a dozen more to do, including two subsequent Julia Kole film musicals, and a muchly needed advance. A week later he phoned Jed with the information that Miss Kole was in New York for a few days. He had the inspiration to send her, by messenger, a dupe of the still from *Love Dance,* accompanied by Jed's two paragraphs of copy, asking for her reaction. Jed's name was on a slug-line of the caption copy. The celebrated lady of film phoned Morgan, indicating her approval, and suggesting that she would be willing to meet face to face with the writer, and perhaps be helpful in making subsequent captions equally apt and suitable. A brief meeting was planned.

Morgan arranged a showing of the musical film *Parade* in the ground floor projection room of their building just before Jed's appointment at the Plaza. The big production number had its full impact on the big screen: Julia Kole leading a parade, her beautiful long legs kicking high; six Julia Koles sliding the glistening brass of every trombone, another Julia pounding the big bass drum. Every face in the crowd was Julia Kole's face, as an overdressed society lady, as a little girl with a balloon, as a young man puffing on a cigar: all the Julia Koles along the parade route cheering and applauding the whirling, baton twirling, radiant Julie Kole. Then the finale: the music cut off, the cheering stopped. But the parading Julia, completely alone, still kicked high along a totally empty 5th Avenue.

"I got goose bumps big as golf balls," Jed scribbled on his note pad.

Jed was enchanted with Julia Kole when he met her in her suite at the Plaza—just one Julia, but that was enough. She looked vibrant and young, filled with energy, as if the high kicks had never stopped. It seemed incredible to Jed that her heyday in film musicals had been thirty, even forty years before.

And she was instantaneously complimentary. "You're a

very perceptive writer, young man." She took her copy of the *Love Dance* still from the coffee table. "How'd you know what I was thinking and feeling? Nobody else ever noticed, not even the director."

"Don't know exactly," Jed said, puzzling it out for himself, too. "Special kind of affinity I have for you. They ran *Parade* for me this morning. What a movie! And I felt I knew you, intimately, in every frame, every one of you. You know what they should have called it? *A Hundred Julias and a Julia.*"

They laughed, both enjoying their relaxed banter. "You think we knew each other in a former life? You believe that stuff?"

"Maybe," he shrugged.

"You ever figure out who you were?"

"I'd liked to have been a lot of people, some kind of writer I hope. Homer? Shakespeare maybe, if I was lucky. Charles Dickens for sure. It would be helpful if I could list all their credits on my ghost resume."

"I know exactly who *I* was in a previous existence," Julia said with mock solemnity. "Shirley MacLaine!"

"You're the most *non*-movie-star-type movie star ever," Jed said. "You're so warm and friendly and funny, too. And you're letting me do all the talking. Isn't the classic definition of a film actor a person who says: 'Oh, please forgive me, I've been talking about myself all evening; let's talk about you for a change: what do *you* think of my acting?' The absolute opposite is true of the generous Julia Kole."

More shared laughter, more coffee poured, as they settled down on the long sofa, clutching opposite edges of the photo still from *Parade*.

"Damndest thing happened on this movie," she said. "The head of the studio didn't understand it at all. 'Why do all those people on the sidewalks look so much like our

Julia? Does she have that big a family? And that terrible final shot where's she's all alone on 5th Avenue doesn't make any sense at all. Get rid of it. Cut it!'"

"Holy God!" Jed marveled. "That's the whole point of it, that's what makes it so great; it has unspoken meaning beyond meaning: we lead our own parades, beat our own drums, toot our own horns. But even if we each consider ourselves the multi-personality of the civilized world, and no matter how high we kick on the march up the Big Street, the cheering eventually stops, the music dies, everybody's parade ends up as a solo act, and we realize the total population of each of our lives is really only one."

"You got it. Write it down. Slap those words under that photo. You know why? Keeping that final moment in the picture was the fight of my life. I had some clout in those days, enough to battle the front office, so I yelled my head off. They ran a preview in Pasadena, for God's sake, and showed me a fistfull of reaction cards from a lot of old ladies. 'Why does Miss Kole try to hog the whole picture?' one of them read. 'Doesn't she want to give any other actresses a break?' Nice snappy stunt, a lot of them thought. Great camera work. Special effects oughta get an Academy Award. 'Screw 'em,' I said. 'Don't you dare cut that finale. Sure, it's sorta sad, sure it makes me the Queen Bee of loneliness, but that's pretty much how I'm feeling at the moment, so that what it's really all about.' Well, they finally caved in, but insisted that from then on the studio would make their Julia more jubilant and less lonely—'Oh, was that what it all meant?'—so they called my next picture: *The Two of Us*."

Jed started to hand her the final photo, still to be captioned. "This one?"

She didn't take it, staring at it for a moment in Jed's outstretched hand.

"Of course. You know damn well it is."

"The guy you're dancing with is Martin Douglas, right?"

"No. It's Mickey Mouse. Rin Tin Tin. Arnold Schwarzenegger. That's like asking if a fella with a bushy white beard, dressed all in red, with a few reindeer hanging around, is Santa Claus."

She took the photo, closed her eyes for the flick of an instant. Jed decided to take a slight invasion of privacy plunge.

"Maybe I shouldn't ask this question, but I've got to. In all the films before this one—when you usually danced alone—is this the fella you idealized as the perfect partner?"

"Dear young, perceptive writer. Why do you have to be more perceptive than is absolutely necessary?"

XXIX.

J ED wrote all 125 of the captions for *The Golden Age of Movie Musicals*. A lot of research was involved, a lot of renting of VCRs, a lot of drafts of each entry. Hell, nobody really likes to rewrite, Jed told himself, but it was goddam necessary most of the time.

And he remembered what one of his favorite writers, James Thurber (who had also haunted the Algonquin) once said: "All my first drafts sound as if they were written by a junior high school scrubwoman. No, I take that back. They sound as if they were written by an *elementary school* scrubwoman."

Rich Morgan congratulated Jed on his professionalism, and handed him an agency contract to become an official part of the "stable." Jed, in turn, congratulated his rented word processor for being so creatively imaginative with mere facts, took it back to the computer store, and bought a shiny new one, entirely his own. Morgan announced that the sixth publisher to see the manuscript had grabbed it, and, with a minimum of editing, was ready to announce a spring publication. "But come in tomorrow, Jed. Like to discuss a possible new project. Maybe two."

When Jed brought the news to Rachel, she kissed him, not once but several times, finally squarely on the lips. So did Kati, who was at her regular perch at the piano, shuffling through sheet music, with a non-stop account of how

Rachel had been coaching her every day, digging up new (to Kati) great old songs, full of melody.

All the celebratory kissing was for yesterday's news. Tomorrow's even happier news from Rich Morgan was the suggestion of a book up ahead solely about Julia Kole. Would Miss Kole be willing? And how would she feel about using an "as-told-to" collaborator? She was hesitant and non-commital in the preliminary phone conversations. Could she think about it for a bit? She'd like to consult with "friends." She perked up when Morgan told her that Jed Jefferson might be available to work with her on the book. But she hesitated again. If she agreed to go ahead, she might want to impose certain limitations on the material. Later on, perhaps, that might cease being a problem.

Would it be possible, Julia asked carefully, to set a future date, some months, perhaps even years ahead, before the book could be printed and released? What date? She wasn't certain, fairly soon maybe, or not so soon. Changing the subject, Julia asked Morgan if Jed would be willing to work on the West Coast. It could be arranged, he said. As for herself, she was fairly free in the months just ahead, with the exception of two benefit performances for Aids research.

The deal was made, fairly rapidly without $300 an hour lawyers dragging their mutual feet: a sizable advance, plus ample per diem for eating money and California hotel expenses for Jed. Rachel invited Kati to come bunk in the guest room of the golden Manhattan house while Jed was off on assignment, and Kati leapt at the chance to be closer to that piano bench.

* * *

Julia Kole was even warmer to Jed in Bel Air than she had been in New York. She hugged him hello at the front door of her home, which rambled over a hillside as if it had grown right out of her garden. Near the top of the hill was a guest cottage, cradled in foliage, but shadowy and silent.

"The hug is for thank you," she said. "They sent me a copy of your caption for *The Two of Us*. I'm grateful to you for not printing your speculation that Mart Douglas is the fella I always wanted to dance with, even if it might be slightly true. One of these days I'll tell you why it wasn't exactly the time, and still isn't, to talk about it in big type."

"Dear Miss Julia Kole," Jed said, "we're about to collaborate, and I think we're going to have a ball, a full dress ball. But you're leading. You're calling the turn. It's your book; I'm only helping to write it. I'm not going to censor myself and I hope you won't censor yourself. But anything that causes you ten seconds of pain, let's leave out. We'll try to be witty enough and pertinent and even entertaining without it. During this collaborative dance, why should I step on your toes? Or forget to brush my teeth every morning?"

He patted the right pocket of his sport coat. "I'm not packing a pistol. This slight bulge is the tiniest, sharpest tape recorder known to man. Or woman. It's not a bugging device, just an attentive ear, so we get down every word you say, without my poking a mike in your face, or scribbling myself crazy. It was a going away, coming back to Julia Kole present: from myself to me. So I don't intend to get in the way. Just talk to Buster here, in my right pocket."

They settled into easy chairs behind coffee cups and Evian-filled glasses. She proposed some ground rules, for

herself, for Jed, for Buster. "I want these as-told-to sessions to be really telling. But how much am I supposed to
tell? I have to be sure not to hurt anybody. I can get
wound up and suddenly find I've said a lot of things I
never intended to say. Does Buster go backwards? Is he
erasable, if I stumble into areas that're none of Buster's
business? Or will you promise not to print something that
shouldn't be printed yet?"

"In the language of high society," Jed joshed, "you bet
your sweet ass I won't."

"You are a gentleman, if not a true nobleman."

And she started talking to Buster, but really to Jed's
eyes, and only stopped for an occasional meal, and for
hugging Jed home to his hotel, and for brushing her teeth
before the sweet silence of sleep.

XXX.

"HOW do you keep from being a victim of the sleaze press?" Julia asked Jed.

"Easy. Don't ever run for President. Don't be a movie star. Don't be a famous athlete; throw away your muscles. And don't even be a relative of anybody famous or notorious: divorce your mother if you have to."

"I think," Julia said, biting the knuckle of her index finger, "that the main reason I agreed to work on this book with you, or to tell Buster anything, is to beat those bastards, keep them from printing anything before we print it ourselves, honestly and accurately and at the right time: from the horses' mouths instead of the horses' asses. Flip on the VCR, Jed. I've set it to a musical number I want you to look at. And I wouldn't mind seeing it again myself."

Jed crossed to the 60-inch TV screen, pushed buttons on the VCR panel, while Julia closed the curtains to shut out the afternoon sunshine. The screen blazed with color as the photo still from *The Two of Us* moved into action: a couple dancing, alone but very much together, in a penthouse setting on Park Avenue with the lights of the city far below. Julia and Jed watched. And listened.

"That's us: Mart Douglas and me. Top of the world stuff. The only film we ever did together. The only musical Mart ever made. He didn't sing very well, so he just *talked* a few bars of the song here and there, the way Rex Harrison did later on. But Mart danced fairly well, at least I thought so, though one critic wrote that he moved more like a hockey player than like Fred Astaire. Isn't that a lovely melody? Not an oom-pa-pa Viennese waltz, but a more modern one, at a time when it wasn't considered mid-Victorian to dance cheek-to-cheek. That's the only waltz I ever danced on screen, alone or with him or with anybody."

The scene on the screen finished with an old-fashioned fade-out.

"Hey. There's a gadget on that thing that lets you freeze-frame. Back it up a bit and get that close-up of Mart looking down at me with that crooked smile of his."

Jed poked at more buttons and the famous face filled the entire screen.

"Now, do me a favor. Turn off Buster, just for a few minutes. I want to talk about that scene, but just to you, and about what happened before it and some of what happened afterwards. Then maybe we can figure out what should be written or not written, and published eventually or not ever published at all."

Jed took his tape recorder out of his jacket pocket and turned it off. "On the table. In plain view. With a flip of the switch, Buster has become electronically deaf."

Julia pointed to the screen. "That scene we just ran isn't about dancing. It's about being in love. And Mart and I were. And we are."

She moved to the screen and touched the motionless picture of that craggy face, creased with smile wrinkles.

"Damndest face ever," Julia said. "First time I ever saw it, except in a movie theater, there was a bagel in its mouth, in the studio commissary on Chicken Soup Special Day; they always used to call that soup 'Jewish penicillin.' I was a not too busty but kinda pretty 17, and I danced into the commisary like a doe in heat, and bumped right into both Mart and the bagel, and it fell out of his mouth and dropped to the floor. He leaned down, dusted off the bagel, and backed away from me, staring, I thought, mostly at my too tight dancing tights. In those days, they called that 'meeting cute,' and I guess it was, but we didn't meet again for a long, long time, on purpose or not on purpose. But I kept a lot of pictures of him in my make-up table drawer, and I'd take them out and look at that face and I suppose I was kinda falling for him, but that was kinda teen-stupid: I was just a beginning chorus kid in a couple of those great musicals they were doing, and Martin Douglas was the top male star of the whole studio."

She touched the face on the screen again, like an admiring kid, who'd just taken a fan photo out of her dressing table drawer.

That's a national monument, Jed thought, a face which belongs on a postage stamp or a hundred dollar bill or carved into Mount Rushmore. There was integrity in the eyes, which presidential candidates wish they had, or were good enough actors to pretend to have. Jed once heard Douglas called both "an actor's actor" and "a no-shit actor" and, incidentally, a no-shit person. George Burns summed it up: "Great acting means being completely honest, totally sincere—even if you have to fake it." Martin Douglas was walking sincerity. No pretension. No self-ballyhoo. Never pretending he was ever anything but Mart Douglas. Thoreau said it a century before: "I'm myself. If I'm not, who will be?"

Julia flipped off the VCR switch, and turned back to Jed. "You blame me for falling in love with him? And wasn't I lucky? Though Mart never said so, I had a hunch he was falling in love with me, too." She pulled open the curtains, stared up the hill toward the little guest house.

"Trouble is, I shouldn't have. And neither should he. He was a married man. Still is."

Jed knew, from all the unprinted rumors, that Martin Douglas could never get a divorce. His wife was a devout Catholic. Elizabeth Douglas grew up in Sacramento society, the daughter of a three-term Republican governor. These days, blue haired and frail, she coveted her privacy in her Pasadena mansion, and shunned any publicity. And apparently, Mart had carefully kept any rumors about himself and Julia away from her.

"I don't keep a diary or a desk calendar," Julia said, "But it's been twenty years, more, that we've been together and not together. It must have been at least four years after the bagel hit the floor that I graduated from being a starlet—isn't that an awful word?—into being a kind of singing and dancing star, with a dressing room trailer all my own. Mine was parked on the studio street in front of Stage 4, and Mart's was about ten feet away at the edge of Stage 3. We weren't doing the same picture, of course, but we became neighborly. Between shots, we'd commute between trailers, sneak from one to the other when nobody was looking, or we hoped nobody was looking." She laughed, still staring up the hill. "Trailers! That's what they call PREVIEWS OF COMING ATTRACTIONS. I guess that's what we were having: previews!"

Julia wheeled around, shouting like a circus barker, vocalizing the large black newspaper type of an imaginary amusement page ad.

"See it soon at your favorite local movie palace! The great epic love story: HIDING IN PUBLIC. Wait a minute! Hold everything! Don't put up cash money at the box-office, folks. For some unknown reason, the film can never be released!"

XXXI

JULIA asked for a couple of days off. She was expecting a "house guest." Jed welcomed the break in their daily as-told-to routine, mostly to get some notes onto paper of their off the record sessions. He swore to himself he'd keep his promise to Julia not to use what she didn't want him to use and try to write without a hint of sleaze.

Back at his hotel, Jed covered every sheet of stationary and even a few envelope backs, jotting down as much as he could of what she'd said. He folded the pages when he finished, and marked the outside: "Confidential." Then he hastily crossed the word out, knowing that was a grab-it-and-read-it-instantaneously invitation to anybody who might possibly come across it. He smiled at his own care-fulness. Who could read his cockamamie shorthand any-how? But still he locked the pages and envelope backs in his suitcase. Then he kicked off his shoes, threw himself on the king-size bed, stuck a couple of pillows under his head, backed up the tapes, and started to listen to Buster listening.

"We've got a hell of a sequence, a montage, I guess you could call it," he heard himself saying to Julia, "of all the Professional Children's School matinees, and dancing and singing coaches, and choreographers ad infinitum, from Hermes Pan to Chuck Walters to Jack Cole, plus sessions with Ruth St. Denis and Bella Lewitzsky tossed in. We could call the whole thing 'A Perfect Pro and How She Grew.' But it's not enough. Oh, we've covered a little bit about life with mama on Yucca Street in the lower depths of Hollywood, that's 'Day of the Locust' territory, isn't it? Buster's heard a little bit about chicken pox and measles, but all I can turn that into is a list or a series of lists, not a book. And I don't know a damn thing about you before the age of five."

He could almost hear her smiling on the tape. "Neither do I. But I don't think I was doing much except wetting the bed and giving my mother grey hair. You know my favorite lines in any book I ever read? The opening paragraph of J.D. Salinger's *Catcher in the Rye*, where he writes something like: "You'll probably want to know where I was born, and all that David Copperfield kind of crap, but I don't feel like going into it."

The tape kept spinning and Jed listened to himself going on much too long about Salinger. Why didn't he shut up and let her talk?

"Not many people know what the J.D. in Salinger stands for: Jerome David! No wonder he only uses his initials. You know, I've always wondered how much most movie people resent Salinger for not letting anybody, ever, make his book into a film. In a way, I admire that. He just wants people to read it, and let the never-made movie run inside their heads."

"I keep rerunning it that way, and I like it. Hope it never passes into public domain. When's that, do you know?"

"Not exactly sure. He wrote it in the late '40s, early '50s, before the new death-plus-fifty years copyright protection, and the old 28 years plus 28 years renewal was still the law. So I guess *Catcher* is up for grabs in the year 2007 or thereabouts."

"Think there'll still be movies then? Maybe we'll just plug something into our foreheads and get THINKIES!"

The dancing star has a brain and imagination and a literary and social conscience, Jed thought, as Julia went on: "What worries me most is that by 2007 nobody will want to make a movie or a 'Thinkie' of *Catcher in the Rye,* or even read it. If there are still books around to read, or anybody wants to read them anymore."

"We'd better get back to the book we're supposed to be writing, or it'll never get read until the spring of 2007, if then, because it'll never get written. Tell me something about your mother."

"Hell of a gal. Worked her ass off all her life so I could take all those lessons on your little list. She was a pastry cook in a couple of California bakeries and sometimes she was a baby-sitter when she could get somebody cheaper to sit with me, and once in a while she was a nursing assistant. She said she'd seen a lot of babies being born, but she never had one of her own until I came along. All the other babies cried, she used to say, not only when they were born, but constantly. I was the only one who smiled. And she said she swore that she'd live and work all her life to keep me happy all of *my* life, to keep me smiling. Quite a mother. I never wanted to divorce *her.* I only wish she'd stuck around long enough for me to pay her back."

* * *

A couple of days after they'd run the number from *The Two of Us,* Jed was invited back to Bel Air. The doors were open to the garden and up the hill the guest cottage was alive with light and the sounds of a baseball game on TV.

"That's Mart up there, as if you didn't know," Julia told Jed. "I hope you and Buster won't object to all that baseball. Gets a little noisy sometimes, but I've learned to live with it. Mart and I have a deal. When he's staying here, he can have all the pro football and hockey and basketball and World Series he wants, and I'll never force him to go to the ballet with me."

"Is he finished with his new film? I've been reading about it."

"He's finished more pictures than any actor, living or dead. And faster. One-Take Martin is his nickname. That's why all the money boys want him, even for a cameo, especially these days when everything's so damn expensive. He gets to the studio or somewhere on location and he says to the director right off, no matter how serious the script is: 'Let's shoot it, kid. I know all the jokes.'"

Jed studied Julia, amazed how she danced with words, doing ballet leaps from one subject to the next.

"I've been telling Mart about you, Jed. He doesn't disapprove of what we're doing, but he's not sure he wants to meet you. Not yet anyhow. Though I wish he would. If this is supposed to be a book about me, let me tell you: he knows more on that subject than I do."

She paused, flopped down on one of the easy chairs, hugging her knees, half covering her face with them.

"But Mart can't tell you any more about my mother than I did. He never knew her, and I guess I never really did either. She was always so busy growing me up, and so was I. And it was always time to go to sleep before we had time to talk, or answer any questions, or even ask them."

"Where was she from originally?"

"I was never quite sure, isn't that strange? My own mother? She was Swiss, I think, or Austrian. But she never talked German or French or Rhenish or whatever that's called. She always insisted that we were U.S. citizens and that meant that we talked English, or at least American.

But she had this warm, sometimes sorta funny accent, as if she were kissing you every time she talked."

"What about your father?"

"He was the main thing she didn't want to talk about. I think she must have felt guilty about something, maybe that she and I got out of Europe when I was about a year and a half old. He'd managed to get the money for us to do it, and the passports and all that, but then he never got out himself. I tried to piece everything together, over and over again, once just before Mama died, but she lapsed into German about how *Gott in himmel* would forgive her for anything she'd done wrong, because she'd loved me so much. Oh, Christ, Jed, I don't want to talk about it anymore than she did. I took a couple of wild guesses, tried to figure out the scenario, as you'd do if you were writing a screenplay or a stage play so that it all made sense. Logically. But it never did. The only thing I could imagine is that my father went back to Austria or Czechoslovakia or wherever he came from originally to try to get other relatives out, and they discovered he was Jewish; maybe he was, maybe he wasn't. But they killed him. Maybe. I'm not sure."

"Did you ever find out where you were born? Was it Switzerland?"

"I think so. I went looking for the place a few years back. But it's not there anymore, unless it just comes to the surface once every hundred years like Germelshausen or Brigadoon. So I guess it doesn't matter."

"It does matter," Jed said. "What was the village or town or canton you went looking for?"

"Crazy name. My mother may have made it up, or imagined it, and I only heard her say it once and not too clearly: she was under sedation and she was crying."

"What was it? What was the name?"

"I'm not even sure I can pronounce it right: Oberplatz."

XXXII.

JED couldn't sleep that night. He'd stopped at a little pizza parlor on lower Santa Monica Boulevard on his way back to his side street hotel, but he couldn't eat. He'd ordered two slices of pizza, bit into the tip of one of them, then spat it into a paper napkin.

Around 2:00 A.M. he decided trying to sleep was useless. He slipped on a sweater, climbed into a pair of chinos, and shoved his bare feet into tennis shoes. He had to walk. He had to think. He took long strides down the quiet deserted residential streets of Beverly Hills, then he began to run. Where to? Away from what? Who the hell knew? How in Christ's sweet name did he ever get dead center of this giant jig saw puzzle? Suddenly everything seemed connected and disconnected. Was he the perpetrator of this puzzle? Or was he just one of the pieces that didn't fit? None of the pieces fit. Some wild game maker had sawed them with so many curves and curlicues that they couldn't be shoved into place without axle grease or Vaseline. Maybe it would be better if it were all left unsolved.

A police car pulled up alongside Jed, politely purring to a stop, no screaming siren, no red light flashing. A tall, blond Beverly Hills cop got out; his partner stayed behind the wheel.

"You in training for the Olympics, Mac? What's your hurry?"

"I was just taking a walk, officer. Had to do some thinking."

"Looks more like a run to me. But nobody walks in Beverly Hills, not at night they don't. Lemme see your I.D."

Jed patted his pockets. "Left my wallet at my hotel." He pulled out his room key. "This one."

"Nice little place. Better get back there and do your thinking in private. Nobody thinks in public in this town unless they're paid big money. Hop in. We'll give you a free ride to your hotel."

Back in his room, Jed still couldn't sleep. He grabbed the tape recorder, backed it up to the last thing Julia had said, a century ago yesterday afternoon.

"I'm not even sure I can pronounce it right: Oberplatz."

He reversed it again.

"I'm not even sure I can pronounce it right: Oberplatz."

The pieces of the jig-saw puzzle, jumbled inside his head, turned into a line from an old song: "Put 'em all together they spell Mother." Maybe he could convince Rachel to do another performance of the Face of Truth. Even if she lied a little, it might put some pieces of the puzzle in place. Though he knew Rachel usually slept until at least 11:00 every morning, he put through a call at 7:50 A.M. California time when it still only cost 35 cents.

"I hope I didn't wake you, dear Rachel."

"What would make you think that, Jedediah? Normally you might have, calling me in the middle of the night like this, but I've been lying in bed, listening to beautiful music by Kati and her splendid new accompanist. All my favorite old melodies, so I feel I'm being serenaded awake. Can you hear them?"

Jed listened as Rachel was obviously pointing her phone mouthpiece in the direction of the golden room.

When the great lady returned, Jed tried quickly to say: "Rachel, I have something important to—" but she plunged ahead. "Kati will absolutely fracture me for not telling her you're calling, but I don't dare interrupt them, they're doing such good work. You know how vital it is to get a true collaborator at the piano bench, and I think we've found one; most accompanists seem to declare war on a singer, as if she were the enemy."

"I'm so grateful to you for watching over her so well while I'm out here in the Hills of Beverly. Now, if you have a minute —"

"She misses you, of course. But so do I, you handsome creature. I'll be sure to tell her you called."

"Rachel. Rachel. Can I ask you just one question?"

"Of course, Jedediah, Ask me anything. Any time. Day or night. *Night or Day*. Cole Porter's very best song, I always thought. Well, go ahead. What did you want to ask me?"

Jed paused. He glanced at his watch, seeing it had ticked well past eight o'clock and the 35 cent rate. But to hell with phone bills; he'd paused because he didn't want to dampen Rachel's morning joy.

"When we first met, and we started full steam on part two of your book, you once mentioned the name of a town, a village maybe, or a canton, in Switzerland. And for some reason you corrected yourself, as if it were a mistake, or you tried to pretend you never said it, or didn't want to say it out loud."

"Did I do that? I don't think I ever did that."

"If I mention the name of the place I remember your saying, do you think you'd recognize it?"

"Oh, I doubt it, Jedediah. That was a long, long time ago."

"Was it Oberplatz?"

A held-breath silence. "It could have been. I don't really remember anything about it."

"While you were there, did you happen to meet any of the villagers? A family named Kole maybe? Kole with a K."

Rachel began to speak rapidly. "The only 'K' I ever knew was Kronheim, and he was there for about ten minutes. I *think* he was there. I'm not even sure *I* was there. Let me think about it some more, and we'll discuss it when you get back to New York. Right now I just want to hear more of that beautiful music. Take good care of yourself and come back soon."

The instant Jed hung up, the phone rang. The hotel operator said a call had come in while his line was busy but that there was a message which sounded fairly urgent from a lady named Julia Somebody. She had said not to call back, that the phones would be all tied up, but asked that Mr. Jefferson come right over.

He tried dialing Julia on all three of her unlisted numbers: they were all busy. Not waiting to shower or shave, Jed simply brushed his teeth, ran a comb through his hair, and started pulling on clothes. He quickly phoned for a cab, saying he'd be in front of the hotel, so come pick him up right away. He normally took the Sunset Boulevard bus to the Bel Air gate and then walked leisurely up the hill to Julia's house. Not today.

Just as the Yellow Cab pulled up at the curb, Jed glanced back at his reflection in the plate glass hotel front. Jesus, he'd put his sweater on backwards, inside out. To hell with it. He climbed into the cab, gave the driver instructions and settled in his seat. A guru in Berkeley a couple of years back, when it was popular to believe gurus, had told Jed it was good luck to put on clothes backwards. My God, Jed thought, today I could win the

Lotto Lottery: I've got everything on backwards, even my jockey shorts!

The taxi tailgated a gardener's truck as they wound up Stone Canyon Road. They stopped just behind the pickup as it pulled into the driveway at Julia's gate. The truck driver had a beeper and the gates opened. An arm from the front of the truck waved for them to follow. When they reached the house, Jed paid the cabdriver and started toward the front door. He glanced quickly toward the truck: the gardener, wearing a perky cap, was glancing over his shoulder as if waiting for the taxi to disappear.

Jed suddenly remembered his sweater was inside out, quickly pulled it off, turned it right side out, and put it back on, neating his hair with a pocket comb.

"You don't have to dress up to get into this place, kid," a voice alongside him said. "Look at me. And you don't have to ring the goddam bell. I've got a key." A startled Jed turned and stared at that incredible Mt. Rushmore face.

The cap came off, the front door opened, and the "gardener" moved into Julia's arms. "Are you all right, Mart?" Julia asked him, as he tossed his cap onto the entryway hat-rack, a perfect ringer.

"Not bad, considering I didn't get any sleep all night."

Julia took his arm and they headed for the garden room. She called over her shoulder to Jed, who hadn't moved out of the front door frame. "Come on in. Mart and I have a lot to tell you."

"Don't just stand there with that what-the-hell's-that-guy-doin'-drivin'-a-pick-up-truck look on your puss," Mart began. "In the first place I wouldn't be caught dead in a stretch limousine: reminds me of a hearse, and I'm still vertical, thank you. I like to drive, not be driven. But all those perpetual star-gazers think I'm breaking some kind of sacred code if they see me driving along Sunset Boulevard on my own power."

Jed was mesmerized into the room by the most disarmingly realistic character he'd ever seen on or off screen. He plopped down at the edge of the couch, his eyes not leaving Mart's face.

"But a gardener? He cruises through Beverly Hills anonymous as a nasturtium, the lucky guy. All the people do is smell the manure and turn their noses the other way. Great part to play; he's been doin' it regularly for twenty years. And he's a hell of a gardener, lemme tell you. Ask the flowers out there. Now, here's where Julia and I need your help. We want you to write the final scene of the screenplay, or maybe it's actually the first scene of a sequel. I don't usually go for sequels, but I think I'm gonna like this one. The gardener gets fired! Or he retires. He becomes a defrocked gardener. But here's the switch: it's a happy ending. Or beginning. 'Cause this guy starts a whole new life, himself at the wheel, and no piles of shit in the back of the truck."

Julia crossed to where Mart was sitting. She sat on the arm of the easy chair and put her arm around him. Then she kissed his head.

"You don't really mean a screenplay, Mr. Douglas," Jed said. "You mean we can use that metaphor in the book Miss Kole and I are trying to get on paper."

"Will you stop that politeness noise? 'Mr. Douglas' was my father. 'Miss Kole' sounds like 'Miss Anthracite of 1948.' She's Julia, I'm Mart. And screw the metaphors. We're going to tell you, and we want you to write, everything: how it was, how it is, how it's gonna be. Everything, Jedediah."

XXXIII.

THEY sat silently at the breakfast table, each sipping the dregs of a third cup of coffee. All the phones had been turned off. The servants had been dispatched to the supermarkets by Julia, who told them to "buy lots of things, shop all day if you have to."

"My wife died last night," Mart said. "In her sleep. This may seem kinda callous, but I'm not unhappy about it. Because I doubt if Elizabeth is. If she's not already sitting at the right hand of God, she can't be more than a few rows back. 'Our Lady of Arroyo Seco,' they used to call her, 'the Patron Saint of Pasadena.' I remember Louella Parsons back in the old days, waddling onto a sound stage, and the first thing she'd ask was: 'How is your saintly Elizabeth? Still doing all that blessed work for Catholic charities!' Louella was right for once: the legal Mrs. Douglas contributed enough for the glory of all the saints, even the ones with unlisted numbers, to get to heaven non-stop on the Concorde. And she lit enough candles to support the wax industry for the rest of this century and the next."

He drank the last few drops of his coffee, waved away a refill. He talked more softly now, directly to Julia and to the silver coffee pot as she put it down.

"We never had any kids, Elizabeth and I, nobody to leave our 'mutual' lives to. And, frankly, we haven't been 'dating' for twenty-one years. Twenty-two. But she was an okay lady, and I never wanted to hurt her. Neither did Julia. There were a lot of things she never knew about, that nobody knew about, we made damn sure she didn't. It would have killed Elizabeth, a long time before last night."

Mart got up from the table. Julia followed him into the garden, as if both wanted to breathe a little sunshine. Jed stood at his breakfast table chair, squeezing the top rung of it. Mart turned back.

"In about two weeks, Jedediah, after all the hosannas and hallelujahs and Hail Marys have been said and all the flowers have wilted on the gravesite, we want you to go to work on the book, all out, full time, about what it's like to be in love. Christ, Julia could win an Academy Award for that. After the way I've second-based her all these years, I wouldn't even be up for a supporting role. You tell about it, kid, with good, honest words. And we'll help you tell it."

Julia walked out of the sunny garden into the shadows of the breakfast room. "And maybe, I'm not sure, I can find the words, or help you find the words, to tell what it's like to have a child of love and not be able to love it really, except at a distance: just trying to love her with lawyers and money and long distance toys and gifts, and that's not good enough."

Jed closed his eyes, gripping the chair top so hard he was sure the rungs were biting into his palms. He was amazed at himself that all he could think was that he could show everybody the stigmata he'd be sure to have, and that they'd all shout at him: "Here comes the tin Jesus! Give me five, for Christ's sake. Hey, how'd you cut your palms?" But Kati's name and her face blotted out the momentary irreverence: KATI! IT'S KATI! MY GOD,

IT'S KATI! AND HERE'S KATI'S MISS HAVISHAM.
AND HER ABEL MAGWITCH.

Jed opened his eyes. Mart came partly out of the garden, but there was still sunshine on that Mt. Rushmore
head, though he was holding Julia's shaded hand.

"It's Kati, isn't it? Kati's your daughter, for God's
sake."

They nodded.

"And all this time, did you know that I knew her?"

"Of course we knew," Mart said. "Why the hell do you
think you're here?"

"To help write your book. But I can't write it now—it's
too goddam coincidental."

"Damn right it is, but *intentionally* coincidental. Now
you've got a lot more to write about. You think our expensive lawyers and our non-snoopy detectives would've let
Kati fly off to New York with you until they found out you
were a kosher citizen? 'Best dill pickle in the barrel' is
what our man-in-Frisco called you, when he found out
you'd quit that sleaze press up there and threw your publisher's own toilet in his face."

Jed sat down. He looked over at Julia. "And then you
must have known when we first met at the Plaza."

"Matter of fact, I asked for you. I was so grateful you
were taking such good care of Kati. I liked the way you
talked, and the way you looked at me. And I knew you
must be looking at Kati in the same honest way. But, of
course, I had to be careful what I said, because we didn't
want Kati to know who we were until it was the right time
to tell her: last night opened the door to that. So in about
two weeks, maybe we can fly to New York together and
start to act out the end chapter of our book. I've been
waiting twenty-two years for that: long time to rehearse."

Jed tried to shake off his disbelief. "This all sounds

like a combination of Pirandello and Kafka and J.B. Priestly and *Alice Through the Looking Glass*. I'm so mixed up I'm not sure who you are, or who the hell I am, or which side of the mirror we're on, or if we've all slipped out of some kind of time frame and fallen down the rabbit hole."

* * *

In the next two weeks, Buster was turned on again, in both meanings of the phrase. Jed was invited to use the guest cottage up the hill, where previously no outsider had been allowed, except a cleaning woman from El Salvador who spoke no English. Mart descended joyfully and permanently, he hoped, to Julia's quarters, where there was a bed slightly smaller than a football field. It could hardly be described as queen size or king size, so they called it "God size."

Mart spent appropriate moments of mourning in Pasadena, happy to return to the sunnier hillside of Bel Air, where he could finally get it all out in the open air, not solemnly, but even with relieved laughter.

Jed was amazed to find the walls of the guest cottage filled with framed pictures of Kati, ages zero to 22. He didn't mind at all being surrounded by Katies, at least pictorially. He kept his promise not to tell her, by phone or letter, that their anticipated Manhattan reunion might be more of a reunion than she expected.

Mart was Jed's guide to the blown up snapshot gallery. "That's the Mother Superior of the convent up north," Mart said, pointing to a framed photo of a serene faced nun, cradling the week old Kati. "I always called her Mother Shapiro, not to her face, of course, because I never met her. Good lady. She sent letters, two a month, to the lawyers, who sent them on to us, and included a lot of these snapshots. And she kept her promise never to let Kati know who we were, or tell anybody, which wasn't tough, because she didn't know herself. I gotta tell you: I'm not exactly a go-to-heaven-quick Catholic myself, and I yell about a lot of things, mostly the morality corset they lace up around us. But I liked Pope John and I liked the place where Kati grew up. On purpose we never got to see her, which was the toughest part for us, especially Julia."

Mart moved on to the next frame, a shot of a very little girl, trying to walk, to take her first steps. A young nun in the picture held out a cautioning hand, as if trying to catch the child if she stumbled or fell. "Julia raised hell when we got this snap. 'Tell the lawyers to tell 'em to let her walk. To let her run, if she wants to. Free. Run free!' And I guess they did let her. And we let her. She's still running."

They moved down the line of frames: Kati at six, messily eating an ice cream cone; Kati at nine with eyeglasses, and braces on her front teeth; Kati at 16.

"Got kinda beautiful, didn't she?"

"Damn right," Jed said. "Even more now."

"I suppose a lot of people in this town would criticize us, if they knew, for not keeping her closer. But, hell, we watched over her, kept track of her, better than most movie people who usually don't have a fuckin' idea that their kids, in bedrooms right down the hall, are on drugs. I got it on reliable authority Kati doesn't indulge. The nuns did a good job."

"Your authority's right on. Jesus, Kati doesn't even drink. And now she's got me not drinking. She's a hot chocolate addict, of course, but there's nothing holy about what that kid doesn't do. More social minded and ecological. For instance, she thinks the Russians should use their potatoes to feed their ballet dancers and actors and singers, and not ferment it all into vodka."

"Let's have a drink on that," Mart said.

"Who the hell took *this*?" Jed asked as he came closer to a nighttime flash bulb shot of himself waiting outside that joint where Kati had her one night gig. In the photo, Kati was coming out the front door. The sign alongside read:

KATI SINGER
SINGER OF THE CENTURY
THE 21ST!

"That was a short century," Jed added before Mart answered his question.

"Friend of mine took that," Mart said. "Sam. His name isn't actually Sam, it's George Colby. Used to be my stand-in whenever we shot a picture in the Bay area. Wasn't very profitable, so he opened up a part time detective agency, and I started calling him Sam Spade. I got the lawyers to hire him to check up on Kati after she left the convent and we stopped getting snapshots from Mother Shapiro."

"I kinda remember him now, hanging around. Sort of a pudgy fella? Not much hair?"

"That's Sam."

Mart squinted at the "Noise Street" photo. "You're a pretty good looking fella, Jedediah. But I wouldn't count on passing a screen test. But who wants to be an actor anyhow? Not a proper job for a grown man." And they laughed and had a couple of fingers each of Russian vodka.

XXXIV.

MART went off to Pasadena to grapple with estate taxes, joint property, and the probate of Elizabeth's will. Julia knew exactly how Mart would handle the corps of lawyers and accountants. "Do it all," he'd tell them. "Get it all settled and done and tell me about it later." Then he'd come racing back to Bel Air."

Julia stretched out on the garden hill and quietly told Jed what happened between spring and Christmas of 1970. And Buster, in Jed's pocket, listened too.

Julia nodded her head upward, indicating the cottage. "That's been our permanent trailer. Not on wheels. Nobody can yank it away and park it beside another sound stage for somebody else's star turn. Those pictures of Kati up there are all I've ever seen of her, never in person since she was five days old. It wasn't easy to do what we did. I wanted Mart's baby. I wanted *our* baby. We discovered my 'condition,' as they used to call it, just after the sexual revolution of the '60s. But Elizabeth hadn't heard about that and Hollywood was still burning the careers of unwed mothers at the stake; it's what they'd done to beautiful Ingrid Bergman when she had a child by Rossellini, right after she'd played Joan of Arc. Everybody said they'd never let her back in this town.

"Mart thought it would ruin my career, but I didn't give a damn about that; I just didn't want it to ruin *his* life, or our baby's. Louella and Hedda, the grandmothers of all gossipmongers, never mentioned in print or on the air that Mart and I were 'going together.' We never did, of course, in public, but they must have known damn well that we were 'going together' at home; somehow they managed to keep their basic bitchiness under control. These days a story like that would scream itself onto front pages, not just of the sleaze press but even of the *New York Times* and the *Christian Science Monitor*. No keep-your-names-out-of-the-papers P.R. man could tone down the big black type they've been saving for the second coming, not with a name like Martin Douglas involved. He'd done a lot more than just dance with that wicked lady.

"I had to go away, on some kind of trumped-up vacation. I knew for how long. But where? How far away? A couple of people helped, tried to make it easy for us. Easier. One was an incredible lawyer, not Elizabeth's. We all scream about lawyers, take them apart, even Shakespeare did. But Norman was an exception. You've heard attorneys called 'The Great Mouthpiece;' he was the great 'Full-of-Silence-Sit-Still-and-Listen' genius of Law, who loved to keep people out of court and out of the headlines. He found us a beautiful sea shack, up north of San Francisco, near Little River, and a country doctor, who had a tiny, white, scrubbed clinic-hospital. He looked like a combination of Schweitzer, Einstein and Dr. Spock. And can you believe he'd never seen a movie in his life, at least not since Charlie Chaplin? So he had no idea we were famous or infamous or the folks down the block, and sometimes we weren't too sure ourselves.

"This wonderful lawyer told this wonderful doctor that this wonderful schoolteacher wanted total rest so she could have the most wonderfully peaceful baby ever. And that's the way it happened, with Mart making frequent anonymous visits to this schoolteacher. They studied their lessons, they did their homework: how to be a perfect father and a perfect mother in the years ahead without ever being there, until they could be there all the time one day soon, in person, publicly.

"Just before Christmas, Mart was there, the moment Kati was born. Five days later, the doctor himself made a second delivery. Their Christmas present of Kati was taken to the convent where Kati grew up, anonymous as they had tried to be.

* * *

The lawyer promised that the child and the convent school would be taken care of financially always.

"So everything happened as planned, except my hope that Kati would inherit what my mother said had happened to me and be born smiling. Kati bawled like a banshee. I guess she had a baby's wisdom: she knew she might have to say good-bye to us even before she'd had a chance to say hello."

Julia stood up, walked around the garden paths. The sun through the trees made beautiful shadows on her face. The rest of her account of her months in Little River seemed more gentle, like the unplotted scenario of a ballet, gauzy, unreal, "Swan Lake" seen through a scrim. The leaps in time were graceful, unhurried. She told Jed about her sunset walks along the strip of deserted beach just below the sea shack, and how she watched the tidewater choreograph the sandpipers' dance. And she talked about the books she'd always wanted to read and finally had a chance to, and the music she listened to, as if for the first time, though she'd heard much of it before, but not really, not like this, when it was filling the hushed, waiting near silence.

* * *

Mart called from inside the Bel Air house, shouting that he was home and that all useless probates should be removed from the body of law, just as a useless prostate gland should be plucked out of the body of a man over 95. "I may change my mind about that when I'm on the cusp of 94," Mart added, as he kissed Julia.

Then he turned to Jed. "You know how grateful we are to you for steering Kati to Madame Rachel's place. We hear she's a great teacher, and I'm sure that's exactly what Kati needed."

"I've always wanted to meet her," Julia said.

"Maybe you have," Jed said slowly. "A long time ago. I wasn't there, of course, so I can't be sure. And you were very young at the time."

"I don't remember. If that ever happened, I'm sure I'd remember."

"I've got a hell of an idea," Jed proposed. "A perfect way for you to meet Rachel again. Or for the first time. Fly back with me. We'll have a reunion with Kati, with Rachel, together in that fabulous golden room, where it's high noon every midnight."

"When?"

"Any time you say. Next week. Next month. You tell me and I'll call Rachel and set a date. We won't tell Kati ahead of time, of course. You've got to come, too, Mart."

"Oh, sure. You bet," Mart said in that special gee-whiz-fellas-lemon-juice-dash-of-bitters sincerity-satiric drawl nobody could imitate. "Tell you what we'll do: we'll bring along camera crews from CBS, NBC, ABC right on the plane with us. And we'll ask Ted Turner in person to bring his CNN cameras up from Atlanta to meet us at the airport. Then engraved invitations to the editors of

National Inquirer and the *Star* to get to Rachel's place ahead of us, so their paparazzi cameras will be all focused when Julia and I enter triumphantly, stark naked."

They laughed and fell into chairs. "I'll go with Jed," Julia said, more soberly. "I want to. We'll do it quietly, and maybe Kati will let her mother bring her home. Home. To meet her father. And when Jed finishes the book, honestly, decently, we can dance in the streets, and we won't care who watches. We'll both be fully dressed, of course."

Mart got up, pulled Julia to her feet, and they began to dance. Slowly. Beautifully. Around the room and into the garden. Julia looked up into Mart's face. Jed, watching, knew that the music of "The Two of Us" had to be whirling inside their heads and that Julia was being held by the man she wanted to dance with for the rest of her life.

XXXV.

J ED phoned Rachel the next morning, waiting until it was the crack of noon, New York time. "But of course I'm awake, dear boy," Rachel said with incredible energy. "Have been for hours. Well, fifteen minutes at least. But my permanent house guest, that girl next floor, is fast asleep up there: Kati's been learning all the good bad habits of the theater. I don't blame her, mind you, for sleeping late, she's been going to plays or musicals every night, not alone of course, accompanied by her accompanist. I'd go along, but I've seen all of them before, last year, five years ago, or even some of them 70 years ago when Mr. Belasco and Mr. Puccini wrote them far better. You know how much I love going to the theater, but I've discovered a new way: seeing it through Kati's young eyes. I wait up for her. When she gets home, she stands in the middle of the living room and sings all the scenes for me and acts all the songs. What a remarkable child, learns faster than I know how to teach her. Tell me, Jedediah, is there some way a very young grandmother type can legally adopt someone as a grandchild?"

"Haven't you realized it's already happened, with no court costs or lawyer fees to pay? Kati's already adopted *you*. You don't know it, but you've become the mother and the grandmother of us all!"

"Dear boy, you continue to chatter and carry on with

the most charming irrelevancies. But I don't really mind, because as they used to say, it's your nickel. Now what exactly were you calling me about? Isn't it the middle of the night out there in the Land of Milk and Money?"

"It's 9:00 A.M. here, dear Rachel, and I've been up and working for at least fifteen minutes. What I'm calling about is: I want to bring Julia Kole to New York with me for you to meet, and for her to meet you. And to meet Kati. If that's all right, just name a time: a week from now, even a month from now, but no later."

"How about dinner tonight? I'd love to meet Julia Kole. That's the lady you've been working with, isn't it? What an exquisite dancer. I hope you're writing her book with the same kind of fluid movement that she expresses so beautifully in her body language. How lucky she is to have you, Jedediah, to tell all her as-told-to's to. That's the whole basis of the Bible, you know. God spake to Moses and all the prophets and later on to Mark and John and Luke and all that crowd, and they simply took down God's dictation, when they weren't busy inventing a new religion."

"I must have been deaf, or not really listening, all this time," Jed thought. "Their tongues, their vocal chords, are connected. All three of them talk alike, with that great energetic rush of language, that mixture of wisdom and nonsense. But they haven't been together, so they can't be copying each other. It's got to be in their bloodstreams, in the linings and synapses of their brains; they've some-how managed to whisper into each other's minds. No wonder: they're all wearing each other's genes."

Rachel had stopped talking. Jed was jarred into listen-ing more closely, as he heard her muttering, half to her-self. "Kole? Kole? Kole? That's with a 'K', isn't it? I'm sure you told me that before. 'K' as in Kronheim."

The tone of Rachel's voice had changed from easy banter to vaguely remembered pain. Jed was concerned that he had caused it. "A while back you asked me if I knew a family or a person or anybody named Kole, a long time ago, in Switzerland. I've been going back, in my head of course, during nights when I can't sleep, to that village, to Oberplatz, to try to find somebody named Kole. Do you know the French expression which is like 'déjà vu' but isn't? What they call 'esprit de l'escalier'—that's what's been going on in my head. Literally it means 'spirit or inspiration of the stairway,' but it really means that you suddenly realize what you should have said after you've gone out a door, slammed it behind you, and started down the staircase, too late to go back. Doesn't belated inspiration happen to everybody?"

"Sure it does. I hope I haven't hurt you or disturbed you or made you lose sleep, Rachel, with all my questions."

"No, no, no. I want you to ask me questions, especially the ones I never got around to asking myself. And I want to ask *you* questions. And tell you some things that are still behind that door I slammed. Because maybe you can help me, help me sleep."

Jed spoke softly, carefully. "What didn't you do at Oberplatz, dear Rachel? What didn't you say?"

After a pause, Rachel spoke simply. "I had a baby. Or maybe I didn't have a baby. Years later, a long time after what happened or didn't happen, I'd keep waking up suddenly in the middle of the night and I'd rehearse all the words I should have screamed at the police or the village officials or at the lying old women who said my baby was born dead, or at the Austrian border guards, or I should have looked harder to find a baby's grave that wasn't anywhere.

"Months and months later, a New York doctor told me it could possibly have been a false pregnancy, that maybe I'd never even conceived a child. I began to believe that, because I had to believe something. And I convinced myself that my delirium there could have included what the old women told me, if they were ever there at all. Or the fairy tale songs I used to sing to my unborn baby, when I was pregnant or not pregnant, walking through the woods even in the rain. And I started to imagine that the whole thing was a fairy tale, most of them are part beautiful, part violent, aren't they? Wicked witches who steal your baby prince or princess. Or gypsies who kidnap your child and ride off on swift horses singing zigeuner songs: that's the plot of how many old operettas? Then I had all kinds of crazy ideas: maybe Kronheim's sister Erna, who was my midwife, might be that gypsy. But Austrians weren't gypsies, only Hungarians and Romanians. Remember that terrible joke, which I shouldn't tell but we need one now, about the difference between a Hungarian and a Romanian? A Hungarian will sell you his grandmother, but a Romanian will deliver."

They laughed and some of the pain disappeared from the telephone wires on both coasts and from the satellite relaying their voices.

"Forgive my momentary trauma, Jedediah, I seem to make a grand opera out of everything. When you mentioned Kole, I thought it might possibly be Erna Kronheim; a lot of people changed their names in those days. But I was wrong, even to think that. She was a lovely lady, full of optimism: she never had a husband or a baby of her own, so she loved and took care of everybody else's babies. I think the Kronheim family might have had a Jewish grandmother, and I wept when I realized that Erna must have been swallowed up in all the German-Austrian terror. But then I kept hoping that she was just part of the fairy tale, too. The End. End of story. End of the fairy tale. Let's not even talk about it anymore."

Jed closed his eyes, took a deep breath. "Julia and I will try to get back there next week. Let us know the best day, the best time. For Kati, too."

"Any day, just so it's sunset time. My favorite time of day. We'll have tea. Tea, hell. We'll have champagne."

XXXVI.

DAVID Belasco and even Ludwig Kronheim would have staged their climactic meeting with tense melodrama, operatic theatrics, the beating of breasts, screams and weeping, the tearing of eyes out of bloody eye sockets. Not this trio. In Rachel's golden room there was calm. Joy. Music. Even laughter.

They held hands, forming a circle, now forever unbreakable. The sunset was everywhere in the room, but it seemed more like a sunrise.

"I wish I could explain how all this is possible," Jed said. "But how the hell do you explain the impossible?"

"You don't have to be Moishe the Explainer," Rachel said. "That's what they used to call an actor in the Yiddish theater, who had to stand up at the end of every play to tell the audience exactly what happened. Or what should have happened."

"We all *know*, dear Jedediah," Julia said.

Jed looked at the three beautiful faces. "But I can't write your book, Julia. I'd be a literary leper. It's all too improbable. Inconceivable. Wildly coincidental. Even if Charles Dickens had written it, nobody would ever believe it."

"*I* believe it," Kati said, the glow of gold on her face.

"Everything is improbable, dear boy," Rachel said, hugging her Julia, who was smiling as beautifully as the day she was born. "The most impossible thing that ever happens to any of us is being born at all. Improbabilities flood around us every day, even before we get out of bed. History repeats itself, all those imaginative historians keep telling us. Why shouldn't family history? As for Mr. Dickens, why don't we invite him back? He'd be very welcome; he could clean up our prisons with his literary broom, the way he did at Newgate and all those pauper prisons. And he'd do a lot more for the homeless than our dethroned President's ever done."

She kissed Jed. "But we don't need Dickens, Jedediah. We've got you. You've brought us together like some catalytic agent. So we're giving you not merely ten percent, but a hundred percent of our lives. Go. Write. Books. A play, too. Not just about us, or for the three of us to star in, though that's not a bad idea. Write it for yourself, because in the theater the playwright is really the star, or should be. Write it for your Grandma Naomi, who taught you how to listen and how to tell stories. And for your Great Uncle Joshua."

She reformed the clasped hands circle. "Just look at us. We're indestructible, no matter what."

They moved to the piano bench, sitting side by side. Jed stood behind them. Rachel began to play.

"You know who we are?" she almost shouted. "We're the illegitimate children of the legitimate theater! Generations of them!"

Jed gently kissed the top of each head. Kati began to sing "Why Did Yesterday Go Away?" Rachel smiled and accompanied her with a percussive rock beat. They all laughed. Then Julia joined in, a whirling, dance tempo echo of the golden days of movie musicals. Rachel ran her fingers up the keyboard in an exuberant arpeggio, and suddenly Sigmund Romberg and Rudolf Friml were back in the room as Rachel's voice blended into the trio with a golden melody. The Vanishing American hadn't vanished at all.

"See? Yesterday hasn't really gone away, Kati." Rachel said. "It's just been on a short vacation. It's back. It's here. And damned happy to get acquainted with Today. And Tomorrow. And the Day After Tomorrow."

Selected SUN & MOON CLASSICS and other internationally-acclaimed publications.

All titles are published in paperback unless otherwise noted.

Bruce Andrews [USA]
  Give Em Enough Rope ($10.95)
  I Don't Have Any Paper So Shut Up ($13.95)
David Antin [USA]
  Selected Poems: 1963-1973 ($13.95)
Rae Armantrout [USA]
  Necromance ($8.95)
Paul Auster [USA]
  The Art of Hunger: Essays-Prefaces-Interviews
    (cloth, $24.95)
  The New York Trilogy [City of Glass,
    Ghosts, and *The Locked Room]* (cloth, $27.95)
Russell Banks [USA]
  Family Life (cloth, $13.95)
  The Relation of My Imprisonment (cloth, $12.95)
Djuna Barnes [USA]
  The Book of Repulsive Women ($5.00)
  Interviews ($12.95)
  New York ($13.95)
  Smoke and Other Early Stories ($9.95)
Charles Bernstein [USA]
  Content's Dream: Essays 1975-1984 ($14.95)
  The Nude Formalism [with Susan Bee] ($5.00)
  Rough Trades ($10.95)
  The Sophist ($11.95)
Jens Bjorneboe [NORWAY]
  The Bird Lovers (forthcoming)
André Breton [FRANCE]
  Earthlight ($12.95)
David Bromige [CANADA]
  The Harbor Master of Hong Kong ($10.95)
Clark Coolidge [USA]
  Own Face (forthcoming)
  The Rova Improvisations ($11.95)
  Solution Passage: Poems 1978-1981 ($11.95)
  Sound As Thought ($11.95)

Ray DiPalma [USA]
 Mock Fandago ($5.00)
 Numbers and Tempers: Selected Early Poems ($11.95)
Heimito von Doderer [AUSTRIA]
 The Demons ($29.95)
Arkadii Dragomoschenko [RUSSIA]
 Description ($11.95)
 Xenia ($12.95)
Dominique Fourcade [FRANCE]
 xbo (forthcoming)
Sigmund Freud [AUSTRIA] (see also Wilhelm Jensen)
 Delusion and Dream in Jensen's Gradiva ($13.95)
Barbara Guest [USA]
 Defensive Rapture ($11.95)
 Fair Realism (cloth, $13.95)
Marianne Hauser [USA]
 Me & My Mom! ($9.95)
 The Memoirs of the Late Mr. Ashley ($11.95)
 Prince Ishmael ($11.95)
Lyn Hejinian [USA]
 The Cell ($11.95)
 My Life ($9.95)
Fanny Howe [USA]
 The Deep North ($9.95)
 The Lives of a Spirit (cloth, $10.95)
 Saving History ($12.95)
Susan Howe [USA]
 The Europe of Trusts ($10.95)
Wilhelm Jensen [GERMANY] (see also Sigmund Freud)
 Gradiva ($13.95)
Steve Katz [USA]
 Florry of Washington Heights ($10.95)
 43 Fictions ($12.95)
 Weir & Pouce ($10.95)
Valery Larbaud [FRANCE]
 Childish Things ($13.95)
Jackson Mac Low [USA]
 Pieces O' Six ($11.95)
F. T. Marinetti [ITALY]
 Let's Murder the Moonshine ($13.95)
 The Untameables ($10.95)

José Emilio Pacheco [MEXICO]
A Distant Death (forthcoming)
Michael Palmer [USA]
First Figure (NORTH POINT PRESS, $8.50)
Notes for Echo Lake (NORTH POINT PRESS, $9.95)
Sun (NORTH POINT PRESS, $9.95)
Tom Raworth [ENGLAND]
Eternal Sections ($9.95)
Leslie Scalapino [USA]
Defoe (forthcoming)
Considering how exaggerated music is
  (NORTH POINT PRESS, $10.95)
Crowd and not evening or light
  (O BOOKS/SUN & MOON PRESS, $9.00)
that they were at the beach
  (NORTH POINT PRESS, $9.50)
way (NORTH POINT PRESS, $12.00)
Arthur Schnitzler [AUSTRIA]
Dream Story ($10.95)
Lieutenant Gustl ($9.95)
Gertrude Stein [USA]
Mrs. Reynolds ($11.95)
Stanzas in Meditation (forthcoming)
Tender Buttons ($9.95)
Robert Steiner [USA]
Dread ($10.95)
Stijn Streuvels [BELGIUM/FLANDERS]
The Flaxfield ($11.95)
Italo Svevo [ITALY]
As a Man Grows Older ($12.95)
Carl Van Vechten [USA]
Parties ($13.95)
Tarjei Vesaas [NORWAY]
The Ice Palace ($11.95)
Wendy Walker [USA]
The Sea-Rabbit ($11.95)
The Secret Service ($13.95)
Mac Wellman [USA]
Bad Penny ($5.95)
The Professional Frenchman ($7.95)
Theatre of Wonders (ed.) ($10.95)